About the Author

Mashingaidze Gomo was born in 1964 in colonial Rhodesia (now Zimbabwe). Third in a family of eight, he was raised in the armed liberation struggle for Zimbabwe. He lived through the euphoria of independence and in 1984 joined the Airforce of Zimbabwe as an aircraft engines apprentice. After apprenticeship, he joined 7 Squadron as an Alouette III helicopter technician and gunner. In that capacity, he was involved in the Mozambican civil war where Zimbabwe defence forces were in it to protect the vital fuel and rail supply lines linking Zimbabwe with the port of Beira from enemy sabotage. After the war, he joined the Airforce of Zimbabwe School of Technical Training as an instructor in the engines trade and stayed there until what was called Africa's 'world war' broke out in the Democratic Republic of Congo. He served on the eastern and northern fronts and *A Fine Madness* was crafted from diary entries he made during that experience. After DRC, he returned to the School of Technical Training and while there, completed a B.A. in English and Communication Studies with the Zimbabwe Open University. In 2007, he retired from the Airforce to study for a B.A. in Fine Arts (Honours) degree (Chinhoyi University of Technology) and to pursue a life in the arts. Gomo is married with three children and lives in Zimbabwe.

D1638247

About the Book

A Fine Madness is a poetic narrative that transcends the physical battlefield to depict Africa at a postcolonial crossroads where difficult choices must be made.

Poetry's capacity to carry unlimited and complex semantic baggage is exploited to give a common soldier's 'cosmic' perspective of the African problem. Flights over the theatre of war become metaphoric flights over African historical experience which time has twisted into a pattern of violence. Mercy missions are depicted as a chase after the ideal of international justice, which the double standards of the new world order have turned into an ever-receding horizon for a destitute postcolonial Africa.

This is a narrative informed by the conviction that history, well laid down, produces patterns that engage an open mind in interesting dialogue. The author painstakingly spreads Africa's colonial past over the neocolonial present to show an intriguing tendency for human tragedy to keep piling on the same sites of struggle, as selfish human interests keep intervening to preclude lasting solutions for everyone's benefit.

Concepts of responsible African leadership, sovereignty, economic independence, democracy, racism and international relations are interrogated in the light of this conviction. Rising political turbulence in Zimbabwe and the chronic instability of the Great Lakes region emerge as recurrent characteristics of the African historical context.

Gomo says of *A Fine Madness*, "It is a refusal to have my experience interpreted for me by Europeans whose kith and kin dispossessed my ancestors. The man on the spot must tell his story in order to prevent the tragedy from being repeated."

The reader will not find this narrative neutral. The personal experience that informed it is not neutral. It is a weapon of war and no weapon of war in the hands of a combatant is neutral. War's atrocities breed revulsion. But revulsion is necessary to initiate fruitful dialogue that will heal polarized communities and help create a more tolerant world.

Praise for A Fine Madness

It is not often that I have read a manuscript from a first time author and was totally bowled over. This read surely reflects what was going on in the minds of many a soldier involved in the DRC Campaign!

Air Commodore Jasper Marangwanda,
Director General of Operations and Plans
(Zimbabwe Defence Forces).

A Fine Madness is a charmed, mad and maddening prose poetry in which an armed man snoops into Africa's history of deprivation and strife to do the painful arithmetic. Meanwhile, the Congo civil war rages on like a monstrous fire, eating and allowing brother and sister to get eaten by the syphilis of the West's relentless desire to plunder. But, as Mashingaidze Gomo shows here, Africa's is a stubborn hope! As you delve through these pages, you hear echoes of Aime Cesaire of '*A Notebook of My Return to The Native Land*' quarrelling bitterly with Joseph Conrad's 'Heart of Darkness' until you are released. Indeed, it is not mad to be mad in a fine way, because you come out of it with useful vistas.

Memory Chirere,
University of Zimbabwe.

A
Fine
Madness

Mashingaidze Gomo

With a Preface by
Ngũgĩ wa Thiong'o

ayebia

An Adinkra symbol meaning
Ntesie maternasie
A symbol of knowledge and wisdom

ARTS COUNCIL
ENGLAND

Copyright © 2010 *A Fine Madness* by Mashingaidze Gomo
First published in the UK by Ayebia Clarke Publishing Limited in 2010
7 Syringa Walk
Banbury
Oxfordshire
OX16 1FR
UK
www.ayebia.co.uk

© 2010 Ayebia Clarke Publishing Limited
© Mashingaidze Gomo 2010

ISBN 978-0-9562401-4-9

Distributed outside Africa, Europe and the United Kingdom
and exclusively in the US by
Lynne Rienner Publishers Inc
1800 30th Street, Suite 314
Boulder, CO 80301
USA
www.rienner.com

Distributed in the UK and Europe by TURNAROUND Publisher Services at
www.turnaround-uk.com

Distributed in Southern Africa by Book Promotions a subsidiary of Jonathan Ball
Publishers in South Africa. For orders contact: orders@bookpro.co.za

Co-published and distributed in Ghana with the Centre for Intellectual Renewal
56 Ringway Estate, Osu, Accra, Ghana.

British Library Cataloguing-in-Publication Data
Cover Design by Amanda Carroll at Millipedia, UK.
Cover artwork by Getty Images.
Typeset by FiSH Books, Enfield, Middlesex, UK.
Printed and bound in Great Britain by CPI Group & Wi___n Reading Be_shire

Available from ___ ISLINGTON LIBRARIES ___uk.com
Distributed in A

The Publisher ___ LIBRARY ___ nding

To Those Who Stand
in Defence of
African Sovereignty

Acknowledgements

I thank all family, colleagues and strangers (now friends) who have stood and hoped with me during this long wait. I am especially profoundly grateful to the late retired Wing Commander Cletus Mafongoya who was the first to read the manuscript and assured me his hunch was never wrong. May his soul rest in eternal peace and be blessed for the good fight he put up for the work to be finally recognized. I salute Air Commodore Jasper Marangwanda for the support he always gave professionally and without reservation whenever I needed it. And, very special gratitude goes to all the strangers who walked into my life and gave it a new meaning, not because we had related before but because there are parts of the African experience that touched them in the same way they touched me: Judith Mupanduki, who committed time and effort to type the manuscript, Dr Rino Zhuwarara, Memory Chirere and Kamurai Mudzingwa (all from the University of Zimbabwe) without whose professional critiques my madness would not have been taken seriously. Fran, who maintains her contribution was only modest, while I know if it were not for her, the manuscript would not have ended up in Nana Clarke Ayebia's hands. And, finding a publisher as committed to publishing the African story as Nana is, cannot be considered a small feat. Above all I want to thank Nana for letting my voice through, for giving me a break and for making my dream real. I find her hope and effort for Africa going beyond measure and it is my sincere hope that it cannot all be in vain. Her bravery must change the world into a better place for the marginalized.

Thank you all. You are no longer strangers to me. You have become brothers and sisters-in-arms in this last ditch fight for Africa.

Thank you all.

Contents

Preface

Ngũgĩ wa Thiong'o

A Fine Madness is really a collage of verse and prose narratives, memories, images, thoughts and characters against the background of the 1998 Congo war following the death of the Congolese dictator Mobutu Sese Seko and the Senior Kabila coming to power. Kabila, a Lumumbaist was a long time foe of the Mobutu dictatorship. Challenged by dissident guerrillas seemingly backed by the West suspicious of Kabila's links to the earlier Lumumba and his avowed leanings towards Marxism and Moism, Kabila is helped by African forces from more than six African countries, the most sizeable and committed to Kabila's restoration being the Zimbabwean contingent. The poet-narrator would seem to be part of the Zimbabwean forces operating from and around Boende, in the Congo. From the air and on the ground he is able to observe and contemplate the chaos in the Congo, which in his eyes also becomes the story of an Africa that has seen so much blood and tragedy. His observations interact with his thoughts and remembrance of Zimbabwean history of anti-colonial resistance and fight for land, from the First Chimurenga war inspired by Mbuya Nehanda to the current land politics in Zimbabwe. Mbuya Nehanda becomes the image of centuries of African resistance to the colonial horror of chambers wrought by the likes of Leopold II of Belgium and Cecil Rhodes of South Africa and Rhodesia.

But this is not a narrative of history. The actual historical figures are not mentioned. These events are tangential to the torrents of images that are conjured by the author's

1

imagination. It opens with the figure of Tinyarei, but soon one senses that this very real almost palpable beauty is really Zimbabwe, Africa and the Black world. Constant are the themes of the horror and loneliness of war; but also the beauty of resistance. Gomo brings little chance encounters to life and then gives them symbolic significance; his vivid description of the landscape; his sheer immersion into the African landscape makes this collage captivating. He can yoke the most contradictory into a searing insight. The camera lenses of a tourist are transformed in his imagination into the telescopic lenses of a machine gun, the clicking becoming the Guevarian staccato cries of machine gunfire; the tourist and the terrorist become each other. Queen Victoria and Mbuya Nehanda are coupled together; one, the builder of the empire of blood and the other the prophetic voice of a blood of passions and hope. Gomo's Africa may bear the mark of tragedy, the heart of darkness of European making, but, out of it, are possibilities if Africa learns to unite and protect its own.

Mashingaidze Gomo's vision might come across as pedantry with the tendency to see history in terms of a monolithic whiteness against an equally monolithic blackness. But this is belied by the fact that, whatever the interests behind the warring forces in the Congo, it is African armies that are pitted against one another; and those who run postcolonial governments are all Africans. He leaves little room for social fissures on either side of the black and white encounter. By subsuming class divisions in Africa under the struggle between two colour monoliths, he denies himself a perspective that might better explain the emergence of postcolonial dictatorships and their actual relationship to the Western corporate bourgeoisie.

But when he lets his images and characters speak for themselves; his eye for detail draws the scene; his sense of

2

irony tells the tale; indeed when he lets us experience the transformation of the physical landscape into that of the richness of life, his fine madness comes tantalizingly close to that Divine Madness that possesses poets and prophets.

Ngũgĩ wa Thiong'o
Irvine
14th April, 2010

Tinyarei

(Give us a break)

The woman I am missing now is a beautiful woman
An older woman aged in beauty
A beauty that hangs on even as age takes its toll
Lingering on like a summer sunset...reluctant to go
A beauty digging in...making a last stand around the
eyes where her smile is still disarming

Those who have looked askance at the wisdom of falling
in love with an older woman, I have always told them
that it is a fine madness
And for those who have only heard and yet not seen, it
remains madness until they see Tinyarei

She is the perfect thing

And then, there are many who have reasoned again and
again that beauty so superlative should be scattered
around or shared...globalized if you like, so that there
cannot be too much power over the hearts of men in any
one woman's hands

And there are also some, surprisingly black too, who
have argued that beauty so superlative is too good for an
African
They have accused Tinyarei of sitting on money and
insisted that she should invest herself in European fashion
magazines
They have insisted to me that Tinyarei should be walking

the streets of London and Paris, signing contracts that
shackle her to European commerce...
And they have campaigned to be the sales people of her
person

And some have asked *kuti, 'Unomupei?...*[1]
Can you afford the things that sustain her beauty and
style?'

As if all African women are invalids...
Beautiful invalids who marry fortunes
As if all African beauty and womanhood should be
relegated to mere aesthetics

Naturally, I have stood at variance with such ideas

An African woman should be as beautiful as she wants to
be and yet not be shared or sustained by men...
And the madness of falling in love with her should owe
no explanation to anyone...
Not even a group of white journalists from a European
fashion magazine

You see...I feel deeply for Tinyarei...
The feeling I have for her is a deep and powerful thing
As deep and powerful as a bottomless sea
A raging, turning and twisting passion, as inexorable as it
is real

A fire that keeps burning, burning and burning like the
Flame of Independence[2] at the kopje

1. And some have asked, 'What can you offer her...?'
2. The flame of independence is a torch that burns on the summit of
   Harare kopje. The flame symbolizes Zimbabwean sovereignty

5

I know that there is beauty that lies in the beholder's eye
A secret beauty that demands that one should look
again...
And then it suddenly becomes so intense that one
wonders how they could have missed it at all the first
time

And then with all that in mind, I know that the beauty
that is Tinyarei's is undeniable to any eye
She is exceptionally beautiful against any imaginable
background
On the streets of Harare
*Pachibhorani kwa*Muda
*Kubanya kwa*Nyandoro[3]
Or even by the Anglican Cathedral close to parliament
I first saw Tinyarei at the inauguration of Chief
Nyandoro, possessed by an ancient spirit of the land
Dancing to life
Whirling in a whirlpool of music and lore

And she could have snapped any eye anywhere
And she sang: *Kufa kunesu machewe*
           Tarisai ndaitwa mukomberanwa garira
           noko[4]

And at Boende, I missed her with a nostalgia that was
like madness
In the solitude of war, in which men marched in
battalions and flew in helicopters, gigantic aircraft and
other quick birds of war... sometimes in combat
formations and sometimes solo, I wandered in the
loneliness of memory... missing her

3. At the borehole at Muda /At the rain shrine at Nyandoro
4. Death is with us for real/Look I am besieged

6

And it was a lonely Boende, with the MI35 gunships
taking off for Bokungu on our arrival from Mbandaka
during the fight for Ikela and rebels were on the run

And, I was remembering the first time I had seen the
helicopter gunships at Kamina...

Two gigantic birds of war that had ridden the distant
horizon to land in a swirl of blades and dust
And men had gathered from all over the transit camp to
inspect the hi-tech aces everybody expected would
transform the face of the war
And one man...a dark-skinned warrant officer, had taken
pride in explaining their capabilities to awed fighters

And now, they shook the earth, rolling down the dirt
runway, one by one, four giants, laden by armloads of
weaponry
One by one, they laboured into the air, dipped behind the
palm trees and were gone...as if they never were

And Boende became a lonely place...
Alone...watched by the bloodstained glare of the jungle
Unguarded by the bloodied presence of the gigantic
gunships

And on the helipad, two Alouette III helicopter gunships
crouched low and small
And a windsock swayed in the wind
A half-hearted bid to repulse the crowding solitude
And I missed her then...

I missed Tinyarei with a wretchedness that was like
madness

A very fine and enjoyable madness

And it always feels pleasant to miss a woman
Sometimes it is even better to miss than to be with her
And at Boende, it felt nice to miss Tinyarei
It felt nice to defy the conventions of a world that has
institutionalized nature into the racist channels of
Western intellect
It felt nice to defy the judgement of a world that has
styled all life to the whims of barbarians
At Boende, DRC, it felt astonishingly nice to be mad at
the whole world

And, in the messing bunker, I introduced myself as
Warrant Officer Class Two Takawira Muchineripi, *alias*
Comrade, *alias* Changamire[5]
And it felt spitefully nice to be all the names the British
priest had refused in Sunday school
He had said Muchineripi was too pagan and suggested
some such names as Amos, Joel or Peter, all of which I
had refused for fear of offending old grandfather who
had given me the name
And, when I chose to leave his flock instead, the priest
had thought I was mad

And, looking back at it all *pa*Boende, it felt so awfully
nice I could have enjoyed refusing his suggestion again
and again and again

5. The name Takawira Muchineripi is an allegory. Takawira defines
colonial bondage. Muchineripi is a verbal challenge to a beaten
enemy if he still has anything else to say. Changamire is a traditional
ruler and also a title of reverence when addressing elders.

And if I had had to refuse it again at Boende, I would
have iced it with spleen because his own name was Father
Dion
And Dion was from 'Dionysus'
And Dionysus was the pagan Greek god of wine and
fertility
And they said that whenever Dionysus visited Mount
Olympus, the gods got pissed, sang, grooved and
romanced all night long because Dionysus always moved
with a good supply of beers

And yet the priest had said my name was pagan, as if
Greek mythology from which they had taken his own
name was Christian
And in my heart, I had said, 'Are you God?'
Because, even if I had changed my name, I would not
have felt like Joel, knowing that I was Muchineripi
Because, Muchineripi, like most African and for that
matter Jewish names was a social statement. I knew that
Jacob, whose name meant 'supplanter' was renamed
'Israel', which meant 'I have fought with God,' after he
had wrestled an angel of God

And, by the same token, my own name was a social
statement...
A slap...
A slap into the face of someone my grandfather had
wanted to spite and like his own name 'Takawira', it told
the story of social strife
Thus, becoming Peter would not have erased the
circumstances I had been born into
Circumstances that were part of me
Circumstances that were family, tribal as well as national
scars, irremovable by name-changing

Because, no black person born into the colonial era was born into peaceful settings

All were born into brutal segregation against which resistance took all forms ... including naming of children to record sorrow and strife ... lest the people forgot

Divine abstraction

At Boende, I looked into the abstract beauty of creation
and saw that the universe is alive
I saw that nature is the same activity replicated on
different levels of a universal hierarchy, from the micro-
world of amoeba, to the celestial explosions of the
universe giving birth to new galaxies
It is love, it is hate, it is restlessness and it is conflict
I saw that nature is beautifully mad and that its madness
surpasses all the madness of mankind rolled into one

I saw that nature is restless
And I saw its restlessness in the planet
And I saw the restlessness of the planet in a storm
A dark, rain-laden cloud that rode the southern sky,
advancing ominously towards Boende
And squadrons of smaller clouds joined the main body in
a rapid falling-in of the forces of nature into a battle
formation against the belligerent children of the earth

And a big commando looked awfully small... alone in the
middle of the helipad, awaiting the celestial invasion
...AK47 in hand

And Zimbabwean commandos are men who walk tall
amongst us
And I know that amongst other fighting forces of the
world they walk even taller

And a big wind wrestled the equatorial jungle
And a Casa crew cast apprehensive glances at the

approaching storm as they prepared take-off...
eventually doing so even as the cloud laid siege of Boende
and a part of it was breaking formation to make haste
for Mbandaka
And the Casa made a rapid climb for a hole in the
clouds, slipped through and was gone
And the cloud closed in and gave chase
And then the storm was upon the town
A dark and violent mob of nature's hooligans
Blind and savage rain, wind, thunder and lightning in
violent mass demonstration, throwing hailstones, pulling
down homes, felling trees, flooding and blocking roads

And a hut was set alight
And I thought to myself that it was the emotional
turbulence of a living universe
And men cowered into their bunkers and watched for, as
at Mt Sinai, God had descended the heavens and was
walking the troubled land

And the gunships flying to Bokungu, I hoped to God they
would circle warily around the celestial forces
And I imagined the Alouette caught up in the same
predicament and shuddered with apprehension
Other aircraft in other parts of the world have been built
to be all weather...
Built to ride the tempest and the hurricane, but the
Alouette was not one of them
And yet the Alouette was a legend in its own right
A versatile machine thrown around a 38kg frame,
economy, experience and guts had adapted it to fight
anywhere and everywhere except of course, the
Congolese storm
And it was legend not to us in Zimbabwe alone...

A visiting Frenchman had once intimated that the
Alouette III was one of the best aircraft the French had
ever built
And now it was a pity that the day of the Alouette was
setting ... outlived and outmoded by the ferocity of
human conflict

And soon, only memories would remain
Memories of distant battlefields and wily guerrillas
Memories of guerrillas who moved from the frugality of
the bush into the cockpit of the legend and used it with
an effectiveness that astounded even those who had used
it against them

Memories would remain of fallen heroes and body bags
Memories would remain of wide-eyed women and
children being salvaged from blood and destruction

Memories of Alouette III *Kommand*-car hardies...
Vamwe vachiri kufamba pamusoro penyika ino
Nevamwe vane tsoka dzakadzima[1]

Memories would also remain of distant places and
strange women, their heads thrown back in merry
laughter... dancing well

And four lightning flashes came in rapid succession,
followed closely by a gigantic burst of thunder
And I remembered video clips of Russians in Chechnya,
their artillery slamming shells into Grozny streets littered
with carrion men and debris
And no side was letting up

1. Some still walking the land/And others who have passed on

14

And I mused at the idea of using lightning in war
If, as myth had it...
If lightning could be used against personal enemies why
could it not be used against national enemies?
And, was it not time Africa institutionalized its
connections to the supernatural to come up with its own
smart weapons without relying on the expensive
requirements of Western arsenals?

Reflecting upon it later, I thought that everybody was
entitled to think whatever they wanted to think

And, out there, where the storm blindly battered the
land, visibility came close, as if to hide the naked fury of
nature, turning and twisting to play out accumulated
tension
And it beat my mind to imagine just how much energy it
must take to burst the seams of nature to throw the land
into chaos
A chaos that was creative anarchy
A revolution which though blind and brutal was also life-
giving because the rainstorm was water
And the water was life
A life that burst onto the land with death in its wake
A paradox?
A paradox that celebrated the divine abstraction of
creation because in a way, nature is the ultimate artist
An abstract artist operating on a cosmic scale, baffling the
finite mind of man through her unorthodox artistry
Like a storm or volcano to sculpt the land
A reluctant sunset to inspire creation
A yellow moon to romance human sorrow
A violent conflict to manifest the beauty of life and peace

And, in the evening, around the kitchen fire, where we
hoped to be given some of the buns the cook was baking,
a tall commando played *mbira*
A rugged tune that sounded incongruously nice to the
Congolese night

And the rhythm was many things that gravitated into a
story
A story about life and death
A story about love and hate
A story about romance and marriage
A story about witchcraft and magic
A story about social strife and rebellion

And, transcended by the rhythm, I thought that it was
also a story about colonial insolence and war
The story of civilization regressing to neocolonial
barbarism
Sponsored gunmen and armed children roaming the land,
wire-locked to a mode of self-destruction
Jaws hard-set against their own livelihood for reasons
their minds were too myopic, too destitute, too selfish
and too inferior to see through

It was the story of carrion men massacred by bullets
treacherously slipped into subverted hands
It was the story of hi-tech and war...
Armoured cars, helicopters, armed men, commandos,
paratroopers and hired guns crawling into gigantic
aircrafts to be airlifted to the borders of human dignity
To the place of the skull
To the weeping place
To prop up and hold African civilization together, where
it was coming apart, dismantled by the insolent

16

champions of Western civilization
And like our own case back home
Like it was the case all over Africa
What was at stake was a birthright
An African birthright!

And around the fire, it was gaunt, homesick men who
hunched shoulders against the cool night and the war

And the tall commando played on
And the tune was a story
A story about Africa
The story of a mother, stripped of all self-respect by
neocolonial barbarism

The story of designer evil, styled to torment and to take
all without moral restraint
The story of Africa standing alone...scantily dressed

A destitute courtesan subjected to the wiles of Western
immorality in which racist legislators vie for a global
moral deviation

And the commando played on
And the crisp notes rested easy on the ear, lulling the
mind into memory lane
And I thought of Tinyarei
And she danced down memory lane...possessed by an
ancient spirit of the land

And she sang *kuti*: '*Kufakunesu machewe*
                    Ndakanga ndabaiwa'[2]

2. And she sang: '*Death is with us for real / Ndakanga ndabaiwa*'

17

And she danced to life...
A lop-sided minuet simulating a predator on a blood trail

And her headscarf fell
And her dreadlocks fell around her face, obscuring her
vision
And she shook them like a lion's mane

And men danced around her...
Traditional men, armed with assegais, knobkerries,
battle-axes, bows and arrows and an old hunter's rifle
And their dance was a war dance
And the spirit of land and rain, Biri naGanyira was
gracing the occasion, shaking to the rhythm of African
lore

And I said to my grandmother, 'Who are those?'
And she said, 'Spirits of the First *Chimurenga*.[3] They
were hard men, such as will never again walk this land.'

And again she said, '*Nyika ino ndeyeropa muzukuru*.'[4]

And I looked at them and it pooled all my mind to
imagine the raw nerve it must have taken those ancient
men *kuti vatore mapfumo nenduni kubva muchengo
chemba*[5] to face the formidable rattle of machine-gun fire
And they must have certainly known that they would die
And that even if they were to survive that war, they
would still die... but they did it
And it was certainly not for themselves, but for us and
for generations infinitely remote in time

3. First war of resistance to colonial occupation (1896)
4. 'Precious blood was shed for this land
5. ...to take assegais and knobkerries from their huts

18

A paper I once read at Mbandaka...an old paper from home had said that a mass grave had been discovered in the hills of Manzou *kwa*Chiweshe...[6]
Ancient skulls with bullet holes!

At Boende, enjoying the nostalgic crispness of the *mbira* song, *Kufa kwangu*...[7] and missing Tinyarei with a lovelorn wretchedness that was like madness, I wondered if those ancient men did not lie bitter and restless... patriarch guardians demonized by children for whom they had faced invading armies in order to retain the God-given heritage of their productive lands
Did the wily Mukwati, who coordinated African resistance...?
Or the mother of that resistance Nehanda, who would not be defiled by the bloodied hands of the colonial priests...?
Did they not lie bitter guardians?
Did they not lie bitter guardians... watching their own pride of race not telling their children their stories and preferring them to be neocolonial slaves rather than free men?

At Boende, hunching shoulders against the cool night and the war, I wondered if my great grandfather's bones did not lie anonymous amongst the bones of the murdered men... restless and un-atoned
I had the picture of big eerie trees hunching their own titanic shoulders over the graves of the murdered men ... their night shadows heavy and thick... forming grotesque figures... sentries that haunted and worried the murdered men, condensing their spirits into burdened

6.   ...hills of Manzou (Mazowe) in Chiweshe
7.   'My Death'

ghosts that occasionally re-enacted their demise for the lonely late night native traveller... influencing them to stop and take notice of the past in order to recognize it as the faulty foundation of the faulty present... a wake-up call to recognize the present and the future as a resolution of an action that originates in the past... to see the future as directed by the present and the past

My grandmother told me that my great grandfather had been a constituent of the traditional army cast together by Nehanda and Kaguvi in reaction to colonial insolence

My grandmother told me that it was an army of traditional men driven by ancestral determination not to commit national posterity into the hands of foreign usurpers, who were a predatory force that returned gestures of good will and welcome with murder and dispossession

At the place of sorrow, in the hills of Manzou, making a last stand against European invaders, the men played *Kufa kwangu* standing up against a destiny of dispossession
And they wondered in rhythm and rhyme why God had forsaken them

And at Boende, in the leaping glow of the Congolese fire, the tall commando also played *Kufa kwangu,* as if by atavistic selection that drew combatants for African liberation to the same rhythms and rhymes

Over a century of conflict stretched between us
And it had been then, as it was still now, a story about land

20

A story about the selective application of the morality of land ownership and the right to life by the champions of civilization

And I wondered how much the African soldier of today owed those ancient men...

I wondered what lessons could be drawn from those traditional sons-and-daughters-of-the-soil who cast together a traditional army to fight a colonial army that was diabolically partisan to the thoroughly evil interests of imperial Europe...a garrison population running an apartheid

Government that sat in parliament to legislate absolute iniquity... *pasina aidzora mumwe*[8]

I wondered if there were no lessons for the modern armies of Africa... any lessons at all to be learnt from guerrilla armies that rose from the ashes of the first resistance and succeeded because they were as partisan to the interests of African people as the settler army was irretrievably and religiously loyal to the evils of apartheid I wondered if African armies should be apologetic about partisanship to exclusive African causes even with national histories scarred by colonial partisanship to unbridled apartheid that was deliberately destructive to the livelihood of the African people

I wondered why African people who questioned the partisanship of African armies to African causes ever

---

8.   ...with no one calling for reason

accepted the privileges and benefits of a liberation
brought about by partisan guerrilla armies

How could they take the benefits of liberation and yet
demonize the fighters!

Eyes are strange

Fire attracts all sorts
Fire is civilization
Fire is life
Fire is social communion
In the dark, fire is a beacon to the lost wayfarer on the road
Fire is warmth and no one remains tense around a fire

And at Boende, it loosened the tongue of a quiet, battle-hardened Special Air Services man
He spread his hands around the fire and glorified the African cause
Saga after saga
The Second *Chimurenga*
The Mozambican campaign
Operation Sovereign Legitimacy

He talked about Altena, Centenary in the 70s[1]
About Maringue in Mozambique
About Kinshasa, Kabalo, Manono

He talked about William Ndangana and The Crocodile Gang
He talked about Chinhoyi
He talked about Mayor Urimbo and Nehanda's pilgrimage into exile[2]

1. The attack on Altena Farm (Centenary) on 21 December 1972 marked the beginning of sustained armed struggle
2. Nehanda's spirit medium went into exile to give spiritual direction to the war. Mayor Urimbo was one of the guerrillas who took her into exile.

And he spoke of ill equipped ZANLA and ZIPRA[3]
guerrillas pitted against a colonial war machine perfected
for deed of malevolence ... prejudiced to see only white
victims in the carnage that a bigoted Ian Smith had
institutionalized

He talked about how most of the early fighters had been
captured and executed but kept on coming, until the
myopic Rhodesians had so much on their hands that they
lost all initiative
And he told of battles to a last man ...
Battles against hi-tech invading barbarians, directing
atrocity from airborne battle stations

And he told the story of Clever Mabhonzo[4]
He said, 'The downing of a helicopter gunship by an ill-
equipped guerrilla standing on shattered limbs is no small
feat

It is divine defiance
It is messianic
It is bigger than life

It is legendary and Africans must not allow their legends
to be dwarfed into ragamuffin villains in Eurocentric
literature.'

---

3. Zimbabwe African National Liberation Army (ZANLA) and
   Zimbabwe People's Revolutionary Army (ZIPRA) were the armed
   wings of Zimbabwe African National Union (ZANU) and
   Zimbabwe African People's Union (ZAPU) respectively
4. Clever Mabhonzo was a ZANLA guerrilla whose fighting prowess
   earned him the respect of Rhodesian forces.

And he said, 'But for a tyrannical and vicious Ian Smith, all that blood would not have been lost.'

And it made me wonder how many African mothers had walked gutted rural homesteads bewildered like chickens after losing chicks to hawks ... their insides somersaulting to the sounds of invading gunfire

How many African mothers had watched Vampire jets dive and distant mountains blow up in smoke ... and had known with heart-rending certainty that their children were no more?

How many African mothers had been blinded by tears, their minds split amok by savage bereavement ... unable to recognize kith and kin charred in gutted villages?

How many guerrillas had raced against a tightening iron net of imperialist forces ... fighter jets, helicopters, spotter planes, bombers, artillery, paratroopers, commandos, Grey Scouts, Selous Scouts, sellouts, mercenaries, secret agents and sniffer dogs, all mobilized by radio relay and rushed to hot spots with satanic precision?
And every battle won
Every battle lost
Every fist raised in a war slogan had been a step closer to a bloodied peace
A bloodied peace!

And the battle-hardened African warrior had been everywhere
He was well read
He knew so much ...

And he talked easily, paling us riders of sky horses into

poor cousins
And we listened, so caught up ... so bereft that we had a
history so rich, yet so unsung ...
So rich that there was no need for Robin Hood,
Christopher Columbus or Vasco da Gama in the nursery
rhymes of our children ...
If only all could be told ...

And, it struck me that the history of African resistance to
European conquest and prejudice should not be left to
myth and ephemeral folk tale alone but in a literary form
inculcated into the mental make-up of African children as
a security vaccine, immunizing black children against
Eurocentric prejudice, subversion and dominance. It must
be known that orature alone cannot hold fort against
purposefully well-documented Western media
propaganda that hypnotizes African children into
zombies donning British and American flag bandanas,
entranced by organized confusion and speaking in
colonial tongues yet surrounded by neocolonial squalor

The history of African resistance must be versified into
nursery rhyme and transmuted into extraordinary art for
academic study by generations contemporary and
infinitely remote in future

The history of African resistance must be subjected to
purposeful study that dissects social issues, baring them
for candid and brutal scrutiny

And it felt nice, listening to him, knowing it felt glorious
only as a story told in retrospect ...
After the hunger
The anxiety and gut-clutching fear

The discomfort of premonitions of tragedy that go with war

And yet, in a way, it was also possible he might have just opened up to hear the sound of his own voice...for, SAS men must be lonely men...lonely stars whose appreciation of friendly company goes far beyond that of ordinary fighters
And in the leaping glow of the Congolese fire, I watched his eyes and thought that eyes are strange
I thought that eyes, which we take for granted as the same in all of us are as unique to each of us as the prints of our fingers
They are also in each of us holes of observation into our inner lives, often revealing more than we would want known
They are video screens that tell the stories of our lives often with ruthless candour
They can chill a spine, challenge an adversary, question, implore and warn...
And this man had eyes like I had never known before
And they told the story of blood and loneliness...
Red blood tainted by strain and howl and groan and iron and sweat and tears

Indicating the *mbira*, he said, 'At Kabalo there was a man who had a set...He was a good player...Very good. When the heavy fighting of the early days subsided, he used to play and it used to be very nice and I think I shall always associate the music with war. Come to think of it, it took the violence of war for me to really appreciate *mbira*. Before that, it had always just been there...a siren they used to lure the spirits of the dead to congress with the living. But not today. Today I think this is the perfect music of our people.'

And then he talked about strange phenomena...
He spoke of how destiny is encoded in vision, dream,
intuition, magic and superstition

He talked about men who do not die...
Mystic men of war, whose magic lures enemies to mortal
combat even when all odds are against it

He talked about how it was necessary to identify and
keep clear of such men...
Somebody always had to die in their place

And he said, 'Such is the way of war...
A blood-letting presence that scourges mankind.'

And then other men spoke and I saw that it is
competition to talk that causes lies
I saw that the concept of the hero has not changed since
Plato and Aristotle
The hero remains a cut above the rest...and the
temptation to be one is irresistible...so irresistible that
men stock the stories of their lives with lies...bits and
pieces of truth and fiction borrowed from the dead and
the absent to turn an ordinary story into a saga that
transforms an ordinary man from Chivi into a hero

We were saved from such by the cook who had finished
his baking and gave us two buns each
And when we lingered around, he said, 'If I give you
everything, what will the others eat tomorrow?'

And he took his things and went away

Show me an honourable destitute

And *Ndombolo* drifted from some place not far off in the
dark
And we drifted to the place...
A place called Club Fulangenge

And we watched the Congolese dance to *Ndombolo*
And there was a woman
A woman called Marie
And they said she was from Goma
A Tutsi from Goma
On the hard-packed earth, she floated like a snow
ballerina ...a victim of civil strife dancing the war into a
rhythmic experience
They said she was from Goma...
And the name had a certain ring to it...
A far, far away God-forsaken place ticking with rebels...
Weather-beaten, war-greased and unruly

And I thought that most Congolese names had the sound
of distance about them...

Boende, Wema, Ikela, Kindu, Kisangani,
Manono...Goma... names that easily roll off the
tongue, enticing and inviting to homesick war-weary
foreign forces, as if there was anything more to them
than mere clusters of thatched adobe, Ndombolo and
weapons outnumbering people

And, it was a poor sort of nightlife they had...
Yet it was exciting in its own equatorial riverfront way...

And I watched two Congolese soldiers do a synchronized
dance, their weapons creaking in time to the music
And I watched a small boy in black float more gracefully
than Marie
And he executed an about-turn that would have been the
envy of the hardest drill sergeant major in Zimbabwe

And a little girl clung to her mother
A little girl in a white dress
A white dress that looked filthy even in the dark
And she reminded me of a piglet I had seen at Kamina
A filthy piglet that had foraged in the murk
And I had felt ashamed for some secret reason I could
not understand

And there were more such children around... some
seated, some dancing around, watching their mothers
catching men... their bottoms being pinched and slapped
randomly by armed men
And they were the soft targets of a wrenching apart of
human civilization...
The figures, the sponsors of neocolonial barbarism were
too greedy to notice
And they hung on, their eyes big and hungry
And their condition was abject poverty

And today I am convinced there is something about
poverty that sucks and stinks
It is like quicksand in a garbage dump

Today I know that poverty accumulates a certain type of

foul dirt and has a way of making its victims look filthy
and greedy and unpleasant to have around
Poverty has cold feet
Poverty is gullible
Poverty is the big sell-out

Poverty wears the moral fabric of a society to a
threadbare see-through clock through which the
attractive valuables of a nation are spied on and made
liable to exploitation

Poverty creates pimps and prostitutes
Poverty sustains slavery

Poverty erodes self-confidence to create a complex of
inferiority and inadequacy and a sense of hopelessness
Poverty begs even when right
Poverty makes the voice of its victims unreasonable
Poverty draws disrespect unto itself

Who has ever seen a pauper being respected or genuinely
welcomed by the rich?
Even when they are responsible for his poverty by way of
dispossession and exploitation

Show me a respectable and honourable destitute and I
will show you European colonial legislators who would
not walk on the same streets as the people they
impoverished

Show me a respectable and honourable destitute and I
will show you whole predatory of European nations that
purported to be civilized and yet would not extend basic
human rights to poor African people

I will show you predatory European nations that purported to be the champions of democracy and yet formed minority apartheid governments that legislated dispossession of African people to create a material need that translated itself to consumer and labour markets to sustain robber nation economies

And, I wonder today... I wonder if it is fair that the concept of world democracy should be viewed through the eyes of those who do not want white people to be the less powerful minorities in black African democracies?

Is it fair that we should view good governance through the eyes of those who wish to consolidate and perpetuate dispossession of Africans by white people?

Is it fair *kuti kana ini ndava kukurira ndinobatwa, asi kana ndichirohwa hapana anobata?*[1]

Is it fair or wise that African people should applaud and be a party to such a cause?
A cause tailored to see future generations of African people permanently dispossessed and future generations of white Rhodesians permanently and unfairly empowered?

---

1. Is it fair that I should be held back when I am winning whereas when I am losing nobody holds the enemy back?

Renal cleansing
and healing pleasure

I would debate everyday
I would debate about getting up...
It was an endless debate

To lie in bed after waking up felt good, but it was also to
be idle and to suppress the bittersweet call to relieve a
full bladder...

A bladder that fills up with toxic waste when one is
asleep and therefore unaware
A bladder that also fills up when one is drinking in the
bar room... getting their judgement impaired
And then, getting out of bed in answer to the call of
nature was also to disturb the pleasant solitude of my
dawns... alone in my memory
Missing Tinyarei
Liking the pleasant warmth that always crept into my
loins with her memory

And I would wonder if she also missed me like I missed
her
Craving to be touched
To be possessed
To be enveloped

To be penetrated
To be one with me
In happiness

In sorrow
In death
Craving to feel pleasantly vulnerable
Wanting to be pampered like a baby

And then I would wince and involuntarily turn in the
sleeping bag...aggrieved by the cold truth that to a
bullet, all targets were anonymous...and I just could
surely die...
Just die like the anonymous comrades we sometimes
picked up in casualty evacuations ...
I just could surely die and become the anonymous dead
man in the stories men tell about war

And it would bother me
It would bother me to imagine that the last sex I had had
with her could have been the very last...
And I had walked away from that day not knowing
And the devil of the thing would be not being able to
remember that last encounter differently from other times
And I would think that destiny must owe it to us that
such last encounters be known before hand...

A man's last sexual encounter on this planet must surely
stand out
It should be worth eternal preservation to sustain his soul
in the afterlife
Nobody should surely want to go down on a mediocre
experience

And I would wonder in case I did really get killed...
I would wonder if Tinyarei would eventually get used to
my not being there

Would she compromise her way of looking at
things...and start doing things differently?
Would she warm up to new relationships with men who
would begrudge her having known and loved another
man?
And would such a grudge fossilize into an abusive
bitterness and a resentment of our children for splitting
their mother between the living and the memory of the
dead?
Would she be punished through abuse of the children?

And outside, the misty Congolese dawn would be serene
An enchanting surreal presence that romanced the soul to
an ethereal peace that belied the violence of war
And, dimly seen from the sea of mist, the radio masts,
windsock swaying in a seemingly windless sky, the
broken down aeroplane 'Mampala' and the two Alos on
the pad would look like craft from a science fiction scene

And then ducks would flatter around the *aeropo*[1] and the
Congolese dawn would become like our own village
dawns back home...cocks crowing, weaver birds
chipping...a woman calling to a child like a mermaid
enchanting a dawn traveller by the river

And it would feel so pleasant to wee on the grass...
Taking aim at a beetle and confusing its sleep-fogged
mind with the saltiness of my urine

1.   ...airport

And I would sanction the speed of the urine ... wanting
the experience to last
And I would think of God and be awed by how He could
have thought of everything ... convert a renal cleansing of
the body to an unparalleled healing pleasure anybody
with urine could partake
And then I would tuck myself away, adjust the sling of
my AK on the shoulder and walk away

The light of Western civilization

We serviced our aircraft and weapons in the punishing
humid heat of the equatorial sun
And nothing in our experience could have prepared us
for the punishment
Not even the geography lessons on equatorial regions in
high school
No amount of lecturing could have done it
One just had to experience it first hand

Yet it had been nice to be young and naïve in high school
Sitting there, listening to talk about exotic lands even the
teachers themselves had never seen and ideas so alien it
was sometimes difficult to relate to them
The geography, history, literature, religious studies...
Much of it sometimes so astonishingly, so
catastrophically irrelevant to our destitution that there
are many good people today...unbelievably many good
African people walking the streets of African capitals
today, jobless and classified illiterate because they failed
something absolutely irrelevant to the African experience

And then other times they had talked about the great
ideas of the French revolution

And the rise of European nationalism
And they talked about legendary white explorers who
discovered an Africa that was dark and chaotic and
inhabited by savage black people who needed the light of

Western civilization, democracy and Christianity
And we read about famous white men of the cloth who
facilitated dispossession and forced labour of poor
African people

And we read about custodians of modern democracy and
rule of law who formed minority apartheid governments
that denied African people the right to vote and chart
their own destiny
And we read foreign literature that addressed foreign
issues
We read Shakespearean works informed by an
Elizabethan view of a God-created cosmos in which order
was imposed on chaos just as they had done on Africa
and history was not a blind chain of events but
providential sequence governed by Western rule of law
that sanctioned their dominance as destiny and sought to
instil a sense of futility in would-be African
revolutionaries

And, social status was accorded on the basis of
Eurocentric education

An educational system of course deliberately designed to
create African people who are groomed in much that is
irrelevant to their African experience
An educational system that deliberately alienated its
victims from the masses from where they would have
come, so that when they went back, it would not be to
foster unity that bred nationalism but individualism that
advanced the capitalist cause

But fortunately, the well-planned evolution of the African
man into a white man's puppet on a string could not

predict the future
A future in which knowledge would become a paradox
A double-edged sword that also created ignorance
An ignorance that knew there was knowledge
An ignorance that would not be satisfied with just being
ignorant but questioned everything, created doubt and
demanded answers

And contrary to imperialist design, some of the educated
elite sampled their experience and compared notes with
the European man's history
And the findings led to war

A war that put the 'messianic' European's commitment to
principles of Christianity, democracy, tolerance and good
governance to test
And they fought with a satanic resolve to preserve
apartheid minority rule that did not extend sanctity of
life to the African people

And the European lost and knowledge was revolutionized
to be no longer the preserve of a lucky few or be designed
to indoctrinate Africans into colonial servitude

And today's African soldier is a man who has studied the
concepts for which he fights
And he knows that Zimbabwe's history has to be told by
the spirits of the First *Chimurenga* who know that no
lessons about tolerance can be learnt from invading
imperialists who beheaded African people for resisting
dispossession and forced labour
He knows that Zimbabwe's history has to be told by the
descendents of the beheaded who know that no lessons on
human rights and tolerance can be taken from a European

community whose collective conscience is so hostile that it cannot be touched by the disturbing awkwardness of having their own dead resting in peace in the lands of those they not only dispossessed but also murdered and denied decent burial

He knows that Zimbabwe's history has to be written by the descendents of Chingaira and Mashayamombe who are yet to bury their dead over a century after they were murdered

He knows that African history has to be written by the guerrilla and the detainee who fought white people's prejudice
The guerrilla who was where it all happened
The guerrilla who knows that no lessons about democracy or human rights or rule of law can be learnt from white people who institutionalized the slavery of African people
He knows that Zimbabwe's history has to be written by villagers who know that there cannot be any honour in the words of former Selous Scouts[1] who impersonated freedom fighters in order to kill innocent African people and to preserve imperialist lawlessness

Today's African soldier knows that African history has to be furnished by African armies who are fighting the regression of African sovereignty into neo-colonial puppet rule tailored to protect the minority interests of capitalist manipulators

1. Selous scouts were a Rhodesian army pseudo-guerrilla unit

He knows true African history has to be written by
African pilots and gunners who fly in to have an eagle's
view of things and to defend African sovereignty and
legitimacy

He knows true African history has to be written by the
commando who is schooled in patience to sustain the
violent company of the invading enemy in order to keep
Africa on track

He knows that African history has to be related by first
hand victims of neo-colonialism who know that in this
day and age and the level of civilization humanity has
attained the European community still grudgingly retains
a savagery that belongs to the darkest side of the beast
world...a savagery with which to deal with African
people

And, on another day, I thought that African history
should actually be designed and not left to providence
and chance

African history should be made by a new breed of
African judges possessed by all the restless spirits of all
the African children murdered by colonialists at Chimoio,
Nyadzonia and Mkushi
Judges who know no other law except the old Law of
Moses...
No other law except an eye for an eye and a tooth for a
tooth

A Mosaic justice that does not let exploiters live and
African victims die
A Mosaic justice that should not allow invading land

grabbers to hold onto even a square millimetre of stolen
land
A Mosaic justice that stands mercurial to neocolonial
duress, not heeding the institutionalized attitude, lip
service and crocodile tears of Western human rights
groups whose human rights are white rights and whose
democracy is European dominance of African people

African history must be made by African judges
determined to re-visit the past to make amends on the
present
Judiciary archaeologists determined to dig up foundations
of racial injustice... reviewing all murders and correcting
social and economic injustices without regret or
apology... Not averse to using law to handle racial
brutality
Not averse to the application of rude, archaic and gothic
justice to oppressors, who are not willing to let go of the
enslaved African

African history must be made in African constitutions
that do not accord human rights to oppressors who do
not have respect for black human rights

African history must be made by hard old men who can
withstand colonialist arrogance and demonization if
posterity requires it of them
Hard old men wise enough to know that strength is not
always in colour, numbers or sophistication but mostly in
being right

A savage peace

And hours dawned and darkened into days and days
collected into weeks
And we waited as all soldiers must wait for orders from
above
And I saw that a time away from home always affords
one time to reflect on issues one cannot effectively reflect
on while immersed in them
Certain issues demand detachment and solitude
Certain issues demand that one should walk away, sit on
a mountaintop and watch the action below

And certain issues demand that one should watch another
person in a predicament similar to one's own

At Boende, a Flame Diners serviette fell from my diary...
A serviette on which I had inscribed a day's introspection
in the diner above X-mex mall where I used to meet
Tinyarei
The diner overlooks Angwa and George Silundika streets
and you can watch the world embroiled in a rat race
down below
You watch ordinary life-weary city people walking down
to their graves
You watch stubborn people hurrying off somewhere,
busy talking to themselves
You watch hipster-bound girls and braided men busy
being other people

Is there light where we are going?
In the X-mex mall Flame Diner, I sit alone and watch the

world go by down below
I have thought many times now...
I have thought that occasionally a man has to sit down
and review his life and today, at the doctor's as I entered
my age I thought that thirty-five is old...Very old
indeed. I thought that at thirty-five a man who cannot
show anything for all those years of rat racing ought to
review his life and make amendments. I thought that at
thirty-five a man should be somebody and yet now as I
look at the world rat-racing down below, I am no longer
sure...
Hundreds of thirty-five year old men and women are
criss-crossing the street below probably hurrying off to
some secret place to take stock of their wretched lives
and to think that they must be somebody by now

At Boende, on our way to the market, a thirty-five year
old man said, 'I will never marry. Why buy the cow when
you can have just the milk?'
And, I told him, 'Then you are surely going to be a silly
old man...
Pot-bellied and desperate...
Proposing to anything that wears a dress
Begging anything to be your wife'

And we toured a market where meat was being sold in
the open and nobody had cholera
And the half carcass of a pig hung from a pole...looking
withered and filthy
And a thirty-five year old Zimbabwean said, 'If the meat
does not sell today, it will be here again tomorrow!'

And the whole market place smelt foul
And hundreds of desperate thirty-five year old men and

women turned the meat this way and that way with
unwashed hands
And with wretched desperation, they bargained to survive
on rotting venison
And to me, in my own very secret world, it felt very
disturbing

And I remembered a comrade who is now late...a
comrade who once spoke his thoughts in a way that was
shockingly disturbing
He had said, 'I think there are two gods in heaven: a
god for white people who blesses them even when they
are being evil to us and then there must also be a god
for African people and he doesn't care what happens to
us'
I remembered that and thought that each time I
remembered it, my faith always hit a snag and little made
sense after that
And, just how could anything make sense after that...?

And, a beautiful woman I baselessly imagined to be
thirty-five passed us and I thought that the scruffy feet
with worn cutex did not belong to that face

And I imagined another beautiful woman who reminded
me of Yondo Sister to be thirty-five
She sat on her haunches as Congolese women do with
incredible ease
She sat on her haunches selling the highly alcoholic
lotoko home brew

And she looked out of focus at all the armed men passing
by... daring them to court

And there were many of us...Zimbabweans, Namibians, Congolese
And one could not be sure who the next person
was...even though they walked and dressed familiar
And some would be enemy agents...fighting against the people
Greedy, psychic invalids singled out by the enemy's calculating eyes
Singled out and promised individual securities amidst stinking poverty

And as we walked away from the foul smelling market, it struck me that war was confusion...
A menacing confusion that scourged mankind
I thought that one cannot separate confusion from war...
It is the propellant...
Without confusion, there would be no war

And I looked back at the madding crowd of wretched people
And they had all turned thirty-five
And I knew there was no way all of us could be somebody by thirty-five
If all people in all the world became somebody by thirty-five, who would be the poor man bargaining to survive on rotting meat?
Who would respond to the populist politician's fiery promise for a better tomorrow?
Who would be the socialist agitating for better wages?
Who would be the Rasta man singing class struggle?
Whose hands would be greased by anti-people Rhodesian barbarians to struggle against their own people...to run around the world telling a hostile and indifferent international European community that that for which

African ancestors were killed by Europeans is not important?
Who would be the moron telling the world that the important thing is a land where the European's grip on the economy is assured ... that the important thing is a land of exclusive European investment?
Who would agitate for a surrogate democracy in which a minority European population calls the shots?
Who would agitate for a surrogate democracy in which white citizens of African states are only a garrison population guaranteeing the survival of American and British interests and the permanent destruction and dispossession of African people?
Who would agitate for a surrogate democracy in which the power of the ballot is compromised by poverty and the duress of invited sanctions and violence?

And yet suppose some individuals are handsomely paid to abandon hope and reason and national posterity and they really come to have individual securities, would that not be synonymous with being buoyant in troubled waters ... waters troubled by a sharp-clawed temperamental monster that can puncture their life-tube any time?

Is it really necessary for African people to protect small enclaves of false security?
Should any African person be happy to be buoyant in imperialist waters?
Or should we not all fight the neo-colonial monster that troubles the water?

Is it fair that we should live under a peace that hangs precariously on the ledge of Western insolence or racist

Rhodesian arrogance?
Is it fair that the condition for African peace should be
silence, poverty, landlessness and dependence?
What kind of peace is that?
What kind of peace is so diabolically savage to our sense
of humanity?
What kind of peace is so barbaric to a humanity it
purports to uphold?

And just what kind of democracy would have four
thousand Europeans whose loyalties lie with our enemies
controlling the means of production in a sovereign state
of thirteen million landless black people whom they all
hate with passions that are demonic?

The horizon

And then one day, need arose for a mercy mission to pick
an ailing comrade from Bokungu and after some
deliberation, we took off westwards, in the direction the
MI's had taken

A lone Alouette
An angel of mercy

And I rested my arms on the aircraft weapon
And I wondered at the transformation of the land below
Transformation from the comparative security of base to
the uncertainty of the jungle
I thought that it was a security derived from mass
habitation
A security derived from numbers

And I also thought that one never really got used to the
transformation. If one did, then it should have ceased to
amaze me back in Mozambique
And it had always seemed sudden then... one minute you
were among loyal comrades and the next, there was just
you and the pilot and the beat of the Alouette and a land
marked by desolation...
The desolation of armed conflict...

Burnt down homes, some still smouldering
Deserted villages running to seed
And then occasionally...
Only very occasionally you would see a man...
A man casting furtive glances at the bird of war

Wondering at the mysterious figures inside
Wondering whether they could be real flesh and blood
Real men born of woman

I know all that because once upon a time, I used to
wonder as well
I know how it feels like to be a village boy in a time of
war...
A village boy caught in an open field with nowhere to
hide
A village boy casting nervous glances at a bird of war,
not knowing what could happen next

And then I became one of them and came to know that
they were real men from somewhere
Men who love and hate and shed tears
Men with as much fear of death as everybody else
Men whose fear is sometimes their only courage
Fear of what African people could become should Africa
sit back and let the zombies amongst her children be
sponsored into self-destruction and neocolonial slavery

I thought all that and watched the jungle stretching to
infinite...meeting the sky at an ever receding
rendezvous...running off together like evil fairies pulling
a dirty joke on us in the storm-infested wilderness
And we doggedly followed them...a relentless beat of
rotors by a bird of war tremendously outsized by a
colossal conflict bleeding itself out in hostile terrain

Somewhere ahead would be Wema and we would be
bypassing it to the left...making straight for Bokungu
And the horizon ran breathlessly ahead, sometimes
resting on a distant rise and misting away at our

approach...
Just like in the fairy tales of lost children and
mermaids...
The story where the voice of the mermaid is always close
but never close enough
Or the story of the night traveller and goblins which
continue to sound the same distance behind or ahead of
him whether he runs, walks, stands still or retreats

Or the story of Africa and the imperial West
The story in which Africa continues to see and hear white
people talking and meting out justice on her horizon

The story in which Africa sees that through a universal
effort in which African people fight and lose life, Nazi
Germans are overwhelmed and human civilization is
preserved
Perpetrators of the Jewish holocaust are hunted down
and hanged and reparations are paid
The Moslem world is accused of and hammered for
sponsoring and harbouring 'terrorists' against white
people
And it would seem that the ideals of democracy and
peace and stability and human rights have a universal
application that is aloof to colour and race
And it is all in the eyes of an Africa whose population
was enslaved and decimated by generations of white
people from Britain, Europe and America
An Africa beleaguered by terrorist groups and opposition
parties sponsored by the same powers to destabilize
African democracies that threaten to overwhelm white
minority influence
And yet when enslaved Africa runs to the horizon of
justice to be compensated for centuries of slavery by

those whose economies were founded on slave labour and blood and colonial pillage, the horizon of justice pulls away
It pulls away from all effort to thwart sponsored terrorism, responding only when it is for the benefit of white people

It pulls away from Africa's calls for universal action against RENAMO and other rebel groups created and sponsored by white people to destabilize African sovereignty

It pulls away from the Congolese cries for reparations for the murder and maiming of thirteen million African people by white Belgians

And the horizon of justice runs breathlessly ahead of a destitute Africa and the evil fairies...the gods of evil can be heard running off together, their derisive laughter echoing and haunting the racist wilderness

And everywhere bewildered Africa turns, the horizon is there and justice is being meted out...only she is too black to have it
Destitution makes her voice unreasonable because poverty draws no respect unto itself
And when the horizon suddenly put up a dark wall of heavy rain ahead of us, the pilot turned the aircraft the way we had come and the horizon was there again and we chased it back to base, mission aborted

Impeccable English
and French

And, Monalisa, the woman clerk at the terminal taught
us Lingala
And, judging from similarities and near similarities of
words between Shona and Lingala, I thought that African
languages must have a common origin. For instance,
nyama (meat) is common to both. *Meso* (eyes) is *miso;*
maoko (hands) is *maboko; tsapata* (feet) is *tsapato* and
rurimi (tongue) is *lolemu*

Considering the distance between Zimbabwe and the
Democratic Republic of Congo, I found the similarities
striking and in a way, confirming our North-African
origin
And I also thought that in a way, a common linguistic
origin must also mean a common ancestry... At least to
some extent

And, as the lessons progressed, I felt that Lingala, like
most other African languages was marginal... marginal
in terms of effective use in a Westernized world
I felt that its development like that of other African
languages too must have been arrested and inhibited by
colonialism which established a diglossia that relegated it
to second place, to be shunned and stigmatized as lacking
class
And that was in effect a security measure on the part of
the enemy...
A security measure ensuring that even if Africans were to

ever remove the shackles of slavery from their ankles and
waists and wrists and necks they would still be shackled
in the mind...
Shackles some of them would wear like gold and
diamond jewellery to be shown off by speaking
impeccable English and French right down to accents on
the streets of African capitals, in homes, in business, in
parliament, in schools and everywhere, even if it distorted
and inhibited effective communication since it is language
that bears the mind and identity of a people
Since much of what any people are and much of
everything any society think are expressed in language
deriving from its capacity to handle experience that is
displaced in time and space
Since the values that are core to the well being of any
people are sometimes expressible and meaningful only in
the language of those people and no form of translation
may translate to the real thing
Since language transmits and is itself transmitted by a
people's culture
And if one is to think of it, is effective thought,
communication and human developmental cooperation
effectively possible without language?
Where would one start?
And how would complex ideas take precisely
transmittable form without precise words to frame them
for transmission between the minds of men?

How would ideas of love, hate, worship, revulsion or
rebellion be handled between people?
How would they exist outside the frame of words?

Is it therefore not tragic to development and the well-
being of a nation to give instruction and to run business

and government in subversive foreign languages which are alien to and cannot be functionally used by the majority of the people...subversive languages that alienate African people, socially engineered to take away their identity and compromise their self determination?

Is it democratic for sovereign African nations to give higher status to the language of the conquerors?

Is it not the status of languages that compromises the power of African liberators when they have to negotiate terms of peace and liberation in the language of the colonizer... knowing exactly what they want to say, but unable to say it with precision because the colonialist language is not equipped to express the anguish of African dispossession? And they have to look up to the conquerors for the precise interpretation of their desires And yet, how can barbarians who have never been enslaved or dispossessed have the words to express the bitter and gut-twisting anguish of the enslaved and dispossessed?
How can they understand our profound desire to dispossess those who have dispossessed us with the same brutality?
How can they understand our desire to disgorge the eyes of those who disgorged African eyes?

Is it democratic that everything meaningful to the people should be done in the alien language of the minority adversary?
Does that not compromise the people's liberty and give the barbarian an upper hand?
Are people free if language inhibits them from filling a medical form or sitting a business interview?

At Boende, taking Lingala lessons from Monalisa, I clearly saw for the first time how it was mandatory that African states break the chains that shackle them to a retrogressive diglossia and reverse it to bring mother tongues into government, industry and commerce. They must see and acknowledge that any change instituted in the enemy's language may only be superficial at its best and therefore meaningless to the *povo*

At Boende, DRC, on the Southern African Development Community (SADC) Operation Sovereign Legitimacy, I was struck by the catastrophic implications of Africa not developing indigenous languages for instruction, industry, commerce and government

It struck me that if the concepts that form our identity...
If the concepts that make us one and therefore strong are founded and carved in our mother tongues, then, woe to the day those mother tongues are allowed to die, because the concepts would be gone too

And, in a world where nature hates vacuums...
In a world where the African has been relegated to second class citizen...
It must surely be tragic to be an African blank and writable CD...just there, available for any programme, even to self-destruct

I thought that maybe the day of the linguistic freedom fighter is now...
To rise up and stop the effective colonization of African culture and to speed up development by imparting knowledge in African indigenous languages through which the majority think and reason most effectively

The wasp is corrupt

And, one day we observed a big wasp going about her business
And the business was building a nursery in one corner of the waiting lounge at the terminal at Boende

And then she must have missed a step, because a piece of mud fell onto the floor and she flew out to fetch a replacement from the puddle where two pigs had been taking a mud bath
And it was a wonder how pigs could not resist puddles, no matter how small
And puddles were a nuisance to us...providing a breeding ground for mosquitoes that caused malaria that killed soldiers
And to pigs, puddles were skin lotion...providing protection from insects and the sun and it was also the breeding ground for the worms they fed on
And to wasps, it was a quarry, providing building material for nurseries

And then, while the wasp was putting the final touches on the nursery, a big green caterpillar started crossing the floor strutting like an ox

And right in the middle of the floor, it stopped as if to consider something and then suddenly turned and came towards my stretcher bed
And I became apprehensive and got up to kick it out of the room
I have known some of these caterpillars to shed

poisonous hair as they crawl over one's back...taking advantage with insolence

And then, even as I got up, the big wasp landed on the caterpillar, which wriggled vigorously as she pumped venom into it...A subversive venom that paralyzed the caterpillar's fighting systems...undermining its will to struggle and it went limp

And then, I called others and we all marvelled at the principles of flight and load-carrying being put into practice by an insect that had never been to flight school

Thrice, the she attempted vertical take-off
And thrice she faltered under the weight of a load that was almost twice her size
And then, to our surprise, she aligned herself with the door and made a rolling take-off, straight outside where she gradually gained altitude and then came back into the room and went straight for the nursery...a mammoth task executed for posterity!

And a Congolese who had also come to observe the drama said something I could not understand and when I asked for interpretation, Monalisa said, 'He is saying that the wasp is corrupt!'

And I thought it was surprisingly well thought out and everybody laughed at the application of human values to the wasp...
The wasp that had taken the caterpillar hostage, to nourish her own descendants

The wasp seemed to have had very definite plans
In the air where she spent much of her life, she had had a
satellite view of everything
She knew a safe spot for her nursery
She knew about the puddle and about the caterpillar
And, all the pieces fitted into her Machiavellian plan

And she had started building the nursery fully aware that
if the caterpillar knew her plans, she would not agree to
them because no living thing on the planet would agree
to be used to nourish the progeny of another living thing
by giving up its own life
So, in the wasp's plans, violence would have to be used
on the caterpillar's life...
As violence was used to enslave the African to nourish
the children of white people
As Rhodesian colonialists legislated forced labour against
Zimbabweans to nourish their progeny

And, reflecting upon it later on, I thought that if
civilization, democracy and Christianity were a
realization of man's rejection of the law of the jungle,
then there must surely be a part of that jungle which the
European community had grudgingly retained...a
savagery with which to deal with African people

And talking about corruption...
What corruption could be worse than slavery?

> Forced labour?
> Minority rule?
> Apartheid?

What corruption could be worse than imperialist
oppressors training and sponsoring terrorists to

destabilize Africa for rejecting their dominant rule?
What corruption could be worse than imperialist
oppressors subverting and arming African children to
commit fratricide and trash their own sovereignty and
heritage?
What corruption could be worse than a blatant refusal to
acknowledge the immorality of having a few Rhodesian
barbarians owning the majority of prime land in a
sovereign state of thirteen million landless black people?

And talking about definite plans...
Were we here not fighting the definite plans of Western
wasps who were building nuclear reactors and aerospace
industries knowing about the DRC's mineral potential in
the sustenance of such ventures...?
Yet not intending to engage in fair trade for them
Plotting instead...
Plotting to kill in order to gain access

So, was Africa not the fat caterpillar?

The guns at Boende

At first there was a single shot
A lone shot whose echo lasted longer than was necessary
An accidental discharge?

They walked on ... towards Club Fulangenge

And then there was a rattle ...
An AK 47 on automatic!

And the radio at Club Fulangenge suddenly went dead
And silence scurried on mysterious feet into the darkest
recesses of the jungle and listened ... its paranoid heart
thumping
And the night stopped on heavy feet and listened ...

And the men stopped too
And listened
And they looked at each other
And they looked stupid without rifles
And it had not seemed necessary

Nothing had happened since their arrival
Nothing had happened when they had carried rifles
Nothing had happened when they had not carried them

Just like nothing had happened between creation and the
first murder on the planet!

And the jungle crouched around them like a frightened
presence, frantically scrounging around for bits of

darkness and tucking them around its gloomy
figure...reluctant to be identified

And more weapons were fired into the night
And lucky enough, the base was close
And they walked back
And they wanted to run
But, they walked back...
Warily...

And they collected their weapons
And one man had left his spare magazine in the tool bag
under the gunner's seat in the aircraft

And they hung around the porch of the terminal
And when tracers started flying from the river, they went
into the trenches

And there was a weapon that was not an AK47 or any of
the light weapons being used in the conflict...
A weapon that sounded strange...haunting the night
into a sleepless state

And the jungle cast fearful glances at the sky and at the
clouds carelessly moving north
Clouds carelessly moving north when things were looking
so bad

The nightmare

And that night, I had a strange dream

We were back in Zimbabwe, on an air task to *Musi wa Tunya*
The place some African locals showed the white man
Livingstone, who then went down in history as having
discovered the falls, which he named after his queen... a
white woman called Victoria
A white woman who signed a paper authorizing her
imperialist subjects to invade a land she did not own
A white woman who signed a paper authorizing her
subjects to enslave and dispossess a whole nation of
African people she had never seen

And, it had made one woman wonder
An African woman called Nehanda
She had wondered how anyone purporting to be civilized
and Christian could take another human being's life so
much for granted
Take away people's means of livelihood...land, livestock,
the right to live and choose a government of their own
choice...do all that and yet still be revered by self
righteous fiendish men who, even as their crimsoned
hands dripped innocent blood sought to baptize their
victims into a faith that condemned murder and
dispossession
Arrogant, self-righteous marauders who would not see
the ungodliness of murder, rape and dispossession

I dreamt that 7 squadron was a flight of angels

And our Alouette gunships made beat-ups over our God-
given wonder whose name some indoctrinated locals
would not have changed back to the local lingua for fear
that it might confuse white tourists
White tourists who were never confused when Rhodesia
became Zimbabwe
White tourists who never got lost when Salisbury became
Harare and Jameson Avenue became Samora Machel,
East and West Germany became one and by their hand
Yugoslavia and the Soviet Union bomb-shelled into
numerous and incoherent states
Those locals wanted the same conceited and literate
tourists not to be confused by the change of an English
name based on a fallacy to an African name that was
original to the place

I dreamt that 7 squadron was a flight of angels of mercy
And that the earth was restless
And we sensed the violent restlessness of the earth in the
violent crash of the falls
And the Devil's Cataract was exhibiting unprecedented
violence
And we felt the power of the earth exuded from there
A charming madness of turbulent water
A turning and twisting
A powerful sense of dissatisfaction
A writhing charge of tragic premonitions

And I saw the restlessness of the earth translate to war
And the falls was a cascade of bodies and blood
And the smoke of the falls was the smoke of burning huts
And the thundering was the gigantic bursts of artillery
and anti-aircraft fire

And the rainbows were a spectrum of multi-coloured
tracers curving from the ends of the earth

And the earth was lonely
Alone, cruising empty space, circled by a magical moon
that scared its canine life silly
A moon that made a tidal effort to pull the water from
the planet's oceans to drench its own arid surface

And then I was alone
And I started thinking that I had a sentimental
attachment to the Devil's Cataract
That therein must lie the link between me and the earth
The solitude
The restlessness
The turning and twisting
The tossing and turning
The tragic premonitions
The almost maniacal desire to be free

And through the soft showers, I saw Tinyarei
And I saw her again through the smoke that thundered
I saw her in a bum-hugging drop-waist the colour of
violet crimson
Our eyes locked for a split second and then with
something like a catch moved on
And I was thinking that crimson was the colour of the
courtesan
How had she come to put it on?

And it came to me that it had been recommended by
photojournalists from the West
Recommended to accentuate her figure and to make it
more photogenic

And in the thunder of smoke and glory, I watched her
walk away
And I tried to stop her but could not
And I actually got close and reached out but grabbed at
nothing
And I stood in the rain...wondering

And in the dream, Azambezi Lodge became Club
Fulangenge
And Club Fulangenge became Makasa Sun
And the discotheque was going
And the Congolese were dancing
And I saw her again...in her violet crimson bum-
hugging drop-waist

And then she was a girl I once dated at Makasa in 86
A girl who was small
A girl who laughed and danced well
A girl who should not have been a whore
A girl called Cindy

And then she was a Congolese, her crimson *liputa* tied
around the hips to accentuate her bottom
And she floated gracefully across the hard-packed earth
of a dusty Makasa Sun that was also Club Fulangenge
And then she became Cindy again...her head thrown
back in merry laughter

And she was a woman for all men
Zimbabweans, Namibians, Angolans, Congolese,
Rwandans, Ugandans...
And there were others, cheering from the edges of the
dance floor...edges that were jungle
And they were civilians with bulging pants

Civilians who were not civilian at all but white men who were tourists not interested in the falls
And they had cameras and wanted to take photos of Cindy, who was also Marie Claire and also Tinyarei in photogenic violet crimson that was also the colour of the courtesan
And they wanted to sell the image to Western fashion magazines

But...their cameras were sniper rifles with telescopic sights
And I was afraid and cried out to Cindy and everybody else that the white men were not tourists but terrorists

But...nobody took heed
And she was going to be shot
And I woke up in cold sweat

And I was supposed to be relieved that it was only a nightmare
But I was not
And it was strange
And I fell asleep again
And behold...two African funeral men dressed in impeccable English gentleman tradition, from tall hat to tailed coat were organizing Cindy's funeral for she was dead...
Dead in mysterious circumstances
And they had violet crimson ties and scarfs
And violet crimson was the colour of the pimp and the prostitute

And people milled around, waiting for Cindy's body, which had been flown to London for a post mortem
And cartons were being flown into the land...

Cartons of false hair, false teeth, false eyelashes, false fingernails and miniskirts that ended where they started
And cases of English spirits were being unloaded from aircrafts

Cases of Johnny Walker with the picture of a 'Johnny' dressed like the funeral men
And youths of the land were drinking it with abandon, undeterred by the prospect of liver cirrhosis, when their bodies would not be able to dispose of foreign toxic waste

And they were full of praise for the African funeral men for being such good organizers of Cindy's funeral

And the African funeral men were proud
And the African funeral men were saying, 'It is the British pound.'
And if it had not been for the British pound, they would not have been able to pull such a feat
Imagine having to put Cindy's body on a British Airways 747 flight to London for a postmortem that could have been done at Parirenyatwa or neighbouring South Africa...
Man!
What a show of affluence!

And they all wanted their funerals organized by those men
And there was a scramble to register for funerals by the youths of the land
And Tinyarei's relatives, armed sons-of-the-soil and the spirits of the First *Chimurenga* were distraught with grief and wanted their daughter's body back

And they were saying it had not been necessary to send
the body for a postmortem in London
They had already been told that their daughter had been
killed by a goblin brought into the village by a clan sell-
out
And all that remained for them was to get together and
rid the clan of both sellout and the goblin
And there was an argument

And the drunken youths who spoke impeccable English
would not listen to reason
They said, 'Please drag us not back into the dark ages.'

And hired mourners who were also a fashion parade of
pious women false from head to toe would not want to
hear about it

They said, *'Zvemweya yerima ndizvo zvatisiri kuda
kumbonzwa.'*[1]
And they made a show of false teeth, false nails, false
eyelashes and false hair that made them false people
And they frowned and pouted very red lips and spoke in
false accents

And the African daughters of African men and women
rejected en masse the colour black
And they creamed their faces to colour mutations of
white women
And the traditional men who were Tinyarei's kinsmen
wondered *kuti chii chainge chapinda muvana vaMhofu*[2]

---

1. They said, 'We do not want to hear anything about the spirits of
   darkness.'
2. ... wondered what had gotten into African children

70

And the white tourists who were not tourists at all but terrorists and whose cameras were sniper rifles with telescopic sights whispered something into the ears of the African funeral men who were also watchmen for white people who were not civilian at all

And the African watchmen in crimson ties and scarfs said to the traditional men, 'Look gentlemen, we cannot defy the donors' will. Can't you see they are making everybody happy. Everybody is drinking and partying and they are worshipping God and you can't start talking about tradition. Do you know just how much all this beer is costing these donors? Can you just imagine how much they have already spent on your daughter's funeral?'

But, the traditional men and the spirits of the First *Chimurenga* were adamant that they wanted their daughter's body back

They could not see the logic of consulting white men who could in no way be experts on African ailments

And the spirits of the First *Chimurenga* were recognizing the white tourists as the children of the imperialists they had fought
And they could not see the logic of a post-mortem in London where Chingaira and Mashayamombe's heads had been taken and never brought back
And they could not see the logic of partying at their daughter's funeral

And it irked the white people who were not tourists at all when the traditional men would not touch the English spirits

And they said to the African funeral men, 'How can we
get down to serious business with some bloody
traditional men in total control of their senses. You ought
to do something, otherwise...'

And they dropped their voices to conspiratorial whispers

And the next thing, the African funeral men and the
drunken youths who were undeterred by the prospect of
liver cirrhosis went violent
And I woke up in cold sweat
And it was morning

The drunken pilots

And late that morning, an Antonov came in...flown by
drunken men
And it was as if they had been going somewhere else
when they unexpectedly happened on Boende and as in
the cartoons, simply dropped the fixed wing aircraft
from the sky into the middle of the runway like a
helicopter
And it swayed this way and that way like a stuntman on
a tight rope
And at the end of the runway it stopped as in the
cartoons and turned back to the terminal
And men disembarked, shaking their heads...
And they were Zimbabweans who had thought themselves
lucky to catch a flight from Mbandaka...Men who had
sought to cut the same journey on the river Tshuapa by
days

A short cut!

And as in Murphy's Law, it had almost become the
longest path between two points...
A light at the end of a tunnel that had almost turned out
to be the headlamp of an oncoming train

And I thought it was like that in life too...
People happening on seemingly good things and
abandoning the normal course of action because it seems
cumbersome
People opting for foolhardy expedience to escape the
demands and responsibilities of necessity

People unknowingly cheering the headlamp of a runaway
dream train at the end of a neocolonial tunnel
People foolishly committing their destiny into the hands
of fools in order to spite those they blame for their woes
because white Rhodesian supremacists say so

And we saw grass caught between the wheels of the
aircraft... grass caught from the edges of the runway

And the pilots, two tall men sauntered out and sent a man
to buy *masangambila* wine from Club Fulangenge
And they found a cool shade under the broken-down
Viscount '*Mampala*' that dozed in the equatorial
sun... an epitome of African procrastination... preferring
to buy
To sell
To rent
To show off
To make do with glitter and not to be real
A relic of ancient European technology marooned in
African backwardness
Obsolete technology reclaimed by con men from
European garbage dumps... dusted and spit-polished to
shackle Africa to technological dependence on Europe
An industrial conspiracy styled to snuff out African
innovation by nourishing the African dream with
European waste in order to diminish the hunger to
develop our own technology
And, once upon a time, the viscount had borne selfish
African snobs to blissful ignorance
Once upon a time it had flown African Neros to play
Western fiddles in European capitals while Africa lay
burning back home
Once upon a time it had borne African puppets to their

second homes in European capitals to lure their
merchants not to trade with Africa as equal partners but
to buy African brothers and sisters, African land and
African resources
Once upon a time it had borne African puppets to
Europe to offer their services as watchdogs for European
interests on the restless continent

And in European hotels
Eating European food
Speaking in broken European tongues
Losing their senses in European cocktails
Getting lost in European brothels
They were pooh-poohed into self-consciousness of their
Africanness and they laughed at silly racist jokes,
concluded suicidal deals and boasted air travel, which
another nation could sanction by control of spares

And they took pride in recounting their escapades
And they wanted to go back to Europe to see a white
courtesan and do it again

And yet if we had consulted even our wizards and
witches on how they fly their trays would we not be
somewhere today ... having a technology to call our
own?
A technology no imperialist could sanction
A technology sustained by locally available and processed
materials and local manpower...
Timber from Mutare
Iron from Kwekwe
Granite from Mutoko
And indigenous skilled manpower
All of which no westerner can sanction

And yet African snobs had boasted of a vibrant industry
they did not own

A vibrant industry of European and American companies
that could translocate to other puppet states
Or be ground to a halt for capitalist reasons
Or only operate on conditions that reduce African
sovereignty to nominal values, making the people at
home ask, 'If the technology was homegrown would we
have fallen into this mess?'

If African governments invested money not in other
people's defective finished products but in industrial
research and locally oriented development by its people
who do not translocate because they know no other
home except Africa . . .
If African snobs would stop sending their children to
better schools in capitalist Europe and start building
better schools here in Africa
If African policy makers would stop getting treatment
from modern European hospitals and start modernizing
the hospitals back home
If African policy makers would start paying local skill the
wages they pay expatriates without grudge
If African policy makers would stop digging rivers where
none exist just in order to build the state of the art
bridges they see in Europe
If Africans would stop inviting sanctions and encouraging
the destruction of the African economy in order to be the
champions and messiahs of its resuscitation

If Africans would stop using a dollar to export and two
dollars to import the same product

If Africans would stop using two dollars to repair a damaged dollar

And, under the broken-down Viscount '*Mampala*,' the pilots drank themselves into *mambaras*[1]
And they waited for their human cargo ... *other mambaras*
...the captured bandits who had caused us yesterday's sleepless night simply because they were drunk

And they were brought in to board the aircraft ...
barefooted and shirtless and under heavy guard
And the guards formed a file on either side of the aircraft entrance
And the guards battered them with booted feet, fists and rifle butts
And the bandits howled and cowered and tried to cover their faces from the onslaught
And some bled
And we watched
And we thought *kuti kusina amai hakuendwi*[2]
And we wondered how a safe flight could be guaranteed if the pilot is a *mambara*
And the flight engineer advising the pilot is another *mambara*

And the passengers are *mambaras* who can hijack the aircraft to an unknown destination

1.   ...crooked people
2.   ...the place without maternal protection should be avoided

Human contact

Few homes we saw in Boende had the air of permanence
about them
Most looked ancient and broken down or likely to
collapse any minute and all human occupation in them
looked provisional, as if the occupiers expected to leave
hurriedly any minute
And yet the paths to those homes would be well trodden
And women would come out of them well powdered,
colourfully dressed and very hungry

And Mami came out of one of those homes with the air
of provisional occupation
A dark-lipped impala
Dainty
Clean-limbed and just as shy

The older sister is the one we saw first
Tall, dark and all-woman
And she could have passed for a Zimbabwean

We joined her somewhere along the road from the
harbour
And she said, 'Kombo nangai Marie.'[1]

And when we stopped by her place when she turned from
the main road, Mami came out of a hut and stood by the
threshold looking orange

1   'My name is Marie

80

And Marie called her and introduced her as, *'Leki
nangai... kombo naye Mami.'*[2]
And we made a date for the evening at YaFeli

And at first I really wanted to go
And then I didn't want to go
And then I wanted to go
And then someone said, 'Do not worry about
language... there is no dictionary as good as the
feminine one.'

And it was true

And she came and we had *primus* beers and we laughed
about how Congolese women had smaller bottoms and
breasts than Zimbabwean women
And it felt nice, just talking and feeling her pleasant
human presence that exuded an intimacy so very
surprising
So very reassuring

And we strolled from YaFeli but to nowhere in particular
And we stood in the middle of a path
And she leaned against me
And we watched the moon
Yellow and luminous

And she pointed to the moon
And she said, *'Mwindi waNzambe'*[3]

And we held hands

2   'My young sister... her name is Mami'
3. 'Light of God'

81

And we stood there for a long, long time
Looking out into the night
Looking out at the moon and the twinkling stars
Strangely contemplating the unimaginable immensity of
the sky...
Of the earth floating in the same sky...
One of millions of other bodies

All of them racing at unimaginable speeds in the same
sky
All of them so perfectly timed there would be no
collisions

And then there was me and Mami...
Two specks of dust
Four tiny eyes looking out into the night
Two tiny hearts torn to pieces by the loneliness of the war

And ours were two tiny minds reaching out into the open
skies up above, awed and run out of imagination

And two Congolese soldiers stopped and watched us
from the shadows and it did not matter to us

And sometimes we abandoned the awkwardness of
language, preferring the definite message of touch
The rustle of breath against the cheek
The wrinkle of the corners of eyes in romantic laughter
The sharp draw of breath as one failed to touch off a
sensual climax

And I had not ever imagined human contact could be so
sweet
So absolutely shattering

And when she said she wanted to go home, I let her
go...

Not wanting the euphoria to end...
Enjoying the chase
Expending it sparingly...like a perishable commodity
Reasoning that the thrill of romance should be nurtured
to maturity like a wine that gets better with age

I felt that the thrill of a foreign romance must be allowed
to linger on like a summer sunset that broods the
company of night

How often has one bedded a lover and immediately felt
that the chase had been infinitely better...?
Felt that the anticipation had been even better?
Almost resented them for not living up to expectation
and fulfilling their human need...?
Said to themselves, 'So, is this just a bright and pretty
face with nothing more to it?'

I let her go...
I let her go and watched her receding *liputa*-wrapped[4]
figure blend in with the night shadows...
An impala stealing through the dark...
Delicate and sure-footed
And I stood alone with the night...contemplating what
it would be like to reach out to her with the light-
fingered touch of romance
To hold her in my arms...
To kiss her to submission

---

4. Liputa is a Congolese cloth

How would her slender-shouldered and delicate frame
feel under my weight?

Would the act of intimacy be a hurried and awkward
incidental?
Would it be an artist's job...one stage blending into
another?
Like the colours of a good painting...
Everything gently rising to a smooth climax
A long letting out of breath
A curling of toes
A reluctance to let go of the moment of truth

And, would I ever want to see her again?

How would it be like to find her disappointing?
A dirty little spur-of-the-moment one-time escapade
colouring the war with a stinking drab

How would it be like not to want ever to see her again?

To meet her on the road and not want to stop and chat
to her?
To see her among other women and be ashamed that she
recognized me?
To see her in the company of other men and yet not feel
jealous at all?

No...

I adjusted the weapon on my shoulder
No!
Not my Mami!
I would want to love her

I would want to love my Congolese impala right into
eternity
I would not allow this romance to degenerate into the
romance such as was between Europe and Africa
A cruel love that felt good only as far as Europe found it
convenient
A cruel relationship in which Europe came and went as
she pleased and by armed coercion, kept Africa in tow

And commandos came on the *Masuwa*
They drifted into base in singles and groups like rogue
lions on the prowl
And again, it struck me that nature was just one big act,
replicated on different levels of a universal hierarchy
The hunt was on and all trails were leading to Ikela
where hyenas were ruling the roost...
The vultures, eagles, jackals... all were headed there

And we went down to the harbour to see the *Masuwa*
aboard which the commandos had come
And it was a big two-story thing
A floating house

And we climbed aboard
And a part of it was in shambles... with cooking fires
burning on the deck... a goat and a monkey tied around
odd places and market wares displayed everywhere

And a woman with a broken front tooth greeted us
pleasantly
And for some curious reason I had the impression that
she must also have a broken heart... broken by the man
who had broken the tooth

And two others... light company by their style, asked for
John *'Peelot'*[5] and it was not the first time John *Peelot*
had been asked for

And a woman I once gave drinks recognized and smiled
at us... ugly and shy like a wild animal
And there was a dark one with her...
A dark one with a huge bottom that quivered like jelly as
she turned to mock all the men stunned by it
And my hands itched to feel it and it was with an effort
that we walked away

And she must have known and enjoyed the effect her
bottom had on men, for, she followed us and we offered
her biscuits, which she refused saying, 'Biscuits are for
children'
And she wanted '7 *Fra*', which we did not have but
promised to give her when we met again

5. 'Peelot' was a colloquial corruption for pilot

The rape

And a storm was brewing

And the flash of lightning was continuous
And thunder rumbled on and on like a wounded animal
And *Mampala* appeared and disappeared with the flashes
of lightning...
Violent glares that rent the shroud of darkness to shreds
Baring rain clouds that were the colour of an inferno

And it reminded me of a painting I did at home
A painting I called, *Restlessness of the Planet.*
And I started thinking that maybe ours was a planet
under stress
A lone celestial craft cruising a vast universe, haunted by
riotious passengers torn apart by the colour of skin
Riotious passengers advancing superficial issues to cover
up intolerant agendas to con the demonized

And we, armed comers from one corner of the ship were
riding miniature craft to rinse peace out of civil blood
and destruction

And the land stood bold and wild and divided against
itself like a wild virgin driven by an inexorable sexual
awakening and yet chained to celibacy by religious and
cultural protocol
A virgin whose 'no' could sometimes also be a 'yes'
A virgin with strong thighs...
Locking them up...
Defying the men of the land to first love her in order to

tame her
To straddle her
To knead her breasts and roll her nipples
To kiss her lips and probe her mouth
To make the insides of her thighs weak with desire
And then to simply spread them and deflower her

And virgin Africa had unintentionally defied Europe and
America to love her
And now she lay sprawled on her back...raped by
exploiters from the West
And they took turns on her
Germans, Americans, British, French, Portuguese,
Belgians...
The whole lot of them
A union and a treaty of economic rapists
And now, she lay hurting and grieving, with no one to
console her

And when her African kinsmen sought to abort the
puppet progeny already restless in her womb, the affluent
rapists demonized and publicized the abortion to the four
corners of the planet

And it was no longer the rape that was evil but the bid to
abort the puppet progeny of the rapists
And *hapana akambotaura kuti yaive nhumbu
yemabhinya*[1]
And the rapists were providing huge sums of money as
pre-natal aid to nurture the unwanted pregnancy to a
healthy delivery of their bastard offspring that would
inherit Africa and hand it back to them

1. And nobody ever mentioned that it was a terrorist-rape pregnancy

And yet I was not afraid

And, in the shadows of the palm trees, I was not
afraid...
And it surprised me
And people shuffled past me...
Armed men of all intentions roaming the night
And women too...
Women whose only defence against the night and the war
was their vulnerability
A vulnerability they carried with them like a weapon of
war
A weapon they carried in the frailty of their bodies
In the beauty of their faces
In the timidity of their smiles
In the knowledge that men had a weakness for the
weaker sex

And they carried it between their legs...
A pleasant vulnerability that saved life by dehumanizing
it into a pawn for a morally awkward security for family,
tribe and race

And nobody saw me...
And none would, if I remained still

And when my catch came, I would know
Dark-lipped Congolese impala...
Nothing like Tinyarei back home, but beautiful all the
same...
Beautiful in an exciting and unfathomable foreign way

And it felt curiously strange that they were both beautiful
Yet incomparable
In my mind, their images resisted comparison
Seeming to prefer to be simply different
And yet good
Each in her own way

And I remembered my grandfather and unsuccessfully
tried to push the memory out of my mind

And it was about similar circumstances as I was in
now...
A similar situation a long time ago
Before my uncles left for the liberation war in the 70s
And my grandfather had thought I was sleeping when he
said it
He had said that the spirit of war required that men
should abstain from sexual congress
And then after a month or so, they had gone with the
comrades and never came back
And nobody had said a thing
And it was only after ceasefire that the older one returned
And he came alone

And now, alone, in the shadows of the Congolese night, I
thought about the younger uncle who had not returned
from war and understood in very real terms what my
grandfather must have meant
Not that I surmised that he must have died because of
women
But I just understood more clearly then
And they always said that the punishment for violating a
taboo is not immediate
And yet I was not afraid

And I perfectly understood the risk I had taken
Coming out alone, without telling anyone
Walking amongst armed men I could not identify... our
vulnerability to what each could do to the other being
mutual and building up to a disturbing security for both
sides

I could be killed...
I could be abducted and it would be a long time before
anybody knew
And, I could meet an armed rival also wanting Mami
and the pride of us men could lead to a gunfight and
death

And worse still, the town could be attacked while I was
separated from friendly forces

And, worst of all, she could be an enemy agent...
A Delilah incarnate set on a blood trail among the critical
riders of the sky horses

Yes... my beautiful Congolese impala who caressed me
with the rustle of her breath against my cheek could just be
that...
And more...
Who can tell what people of flesh and blood are capable of
doing?

And...

Alone, in the shadows of the Congolese night, I saw then
how sex could compromise any struggle
Originally, I had seen grandfather's talk only as divine
fiat, intended to groom a moral responsibility to curtail

indulgences that might compromise the security of
fighters...
Indulgencies that might compromise the moral standing
of fighters in the eyes of the masses to whom the women
would be daughters, wives and mothers...

I saw then how sexual irresponsibility could trash any
revolution...because no population supports sexually
irresponsible fighters who sleep with their mothers and
wives, no matter what the cause
And I also saw that even when stripped of all spiritual
connotations, the advice stood out as very practical
advice meant to keep guerrillas alive
And I saw how a beautiful face pulled down a fighter's
guard, exposing one to imminent death
It had already pulled down my defence as it had once
pulled down Samson's

And yet I was not afraid
And that was the devil of the thing!

And when she finally came, it was from a direction I had
not expected...
One minute she was not there and the next, close to my
ear, a soft voice said, 'Mbote,'[1] and my heart skipped a
beat
And, at a loss of what to say, I drew her close and found
her mouth
And, feet shuffled past us and somewhere in the night, a
Namibian soldier threatened someone

1. 'How are you?

93

And I shut my eyes and forgot the world as all tension
eased from my body...melted by her closeness
And I had wanted to do this in the afternoon at YaFeli
when she had stood very close to me and everybody had
seemed to be looking away...
But I had deliberated too long and the moment had
passed

And a long time later, coming from escorting her, I
refused to imagine that I could simply be a food and
security convenience to Mami

And yet what could any practical girl do, who wanted to
survive?
Was the choice between starvation and death on the one
hand and the immorality of a sexual relationship she
might by chance even enjoy on the other hand...Was
such a choice a debatable one?
Would the alternative of sleeping with an armed man
who might, or might not get away with killing her and
her people be a hard one for a woman?

Monalisa, the woman clerk at the terminal...
The woman with whom we had become friends had only
yesterday asked me what I would do if I were to see her
sitting with her rebel brother
And without thinking I had said I would shoot them
both and she had looked at me with disbelief and sworn
that she would never forgive me if that happened

And now, reflecting upon it alone, I wondered if it was
human shame and weakness that led beautiful women
into the beds of the armed and powerful men of the
land

Was it ordained human weakness that would turn Mami and Monalisa into the Congolese Rahabs, Ruths and Esthers of the Congolese people of Boende?

Toxic waste and
songs of war

And I awoke at dawn
And the Congolese dawn was divine
A serene divinity that seemed polar-opposite to the
violence of war
A misty martian affair that I had come to look forward to

Everyday I enjoyed scavenging toxic waste from my body
Everyday I peed on the dewy grass
Everyday I remembered an old man we once bathed with
in the river *kwa*Chihota when we were young
An old man who had talked about the pleasure of peeing

And it had sounded crude, coming from a 'wicked' old
man
But now I thought that it must take age to acknowledge
and appreciate the beauty and raw candour of such
crudeness
It must take maturity to appreciate the pleasure of peeing
to rid the body of toxic waste

And Africa must pee imperialist Europe and America
Africa must take pleasure in peeing neo-colonialist
Europe and America into the dirt
In its dawn of realization that Western justice is not blind
but partial, Africa must wrest her destiny from
exploitative hands and taste the absolute beauty of
rebellion against neocolonial dictatorship and double
standards

And on that day, the Congolese dawn bore the voices of
Zimbabwe freedom fighters
And it was a song of war...invoking legends of
Zimbabwean liberation to bless Zimbabwean heroes
And the serene Congolese dawn bore it on delicate hands
and carried it far into the mist-enchanted jungle,
modulating it into a nostalgic crispness that transcended
the mind

And I peed on the dewy grass
And I peed into a carpeted hole where a tarantula lived,
having displaced whatever had dug the hole as white
people had displaced African people from their lands
And it came out running and reared on hind feet to show
me sharp fangs, which I ignored and kept drenching it
and enjoying the punishment until it disappeared into the
tall grass
And I ran out of urine

And I stood in the Congolese dawn, listening to the
commando song receding into the distance
And I thought that to sing was good

Song fosters unity...
It demands that one man raise his voice in lead
And that the singular voices of the rest should unite and
rally around that pillar of voice, reaching out cohesive
hands of rhythm and rhyme
Gravitating into anchor around it

And for once, people are one and they are reluctant to
split for, who wants to break a good rhythm?
Who wants to break a rhyme?
Who is selfish enough to want to take their voice away

from a good song?
Who wants to listen to a good song limping into discord,
invalidated by their own refusal to provide a supporting
foot?
Where, upon this planet is a combatant for good causes
who does not want to run in time with a song that
glorifies their cause?

Alone and enchanted by the Congolese dawn, I saw then
why it was necessary that each nation should have its
own song... at least one song everybody should know
An anthem whose rhythms and rhymes only a fool
should want to break
A song around which all the voices of the land should
rally, making the whole nation one and reluctant to split
A song that should eternalize nationhood and forever pay
reverence to the founding heroes of that nation

And Africa must have its own one song...
A plea to the God of heaven and earth, to guard black
children against the racist indulgences of the West

'Kufa kunesu machewe...'
(Death is with us for real)

And for me, the euphoria of song carried over to
breakfast
And over breakfast, in the non commissioned officers'
(NCOs) messing bunker, freedom fighters talked about
Kabalo Bridge and the standoff that had hung on hair-
raising mortal combat

And they talked wistfully...
About life and about mortality
About a corporal with a machinegun
About a corporal and a private who had once saved the
day...
The day the rebels might have broken the stalemate
And they talked wistfully as men talk who have walked
the company of death...
Men who have known that death has descended onto the
land and keeps watch, closing in on the alert and the
unwary alike...

And I asked the tall commando to lend me his *mbira* for
the morning
And one of the men on transit said he carried a set in his
bags and he offered to play with either of us and I opted
out... preferring to listen instead

To listen is better, especially if it is to listen to good players
It gives one time to savour the music without the
distraction of involvement

100

And so they played...pitted against each other in the
messing pit

And at first it was the lead player alone...the man on
transit
A stubborn-looking, wiry traditional man with strong
hands
And the tune of his choice was a wistful one...
A migration of sound from the darkest recesses of the
race psych...tentatively descending the broken hills of
African experience into the valley of neocolonial conflict
below...
The African Armageddon

And the tall commando stalked him...with evil
intentions
And he kept to the shadows waiting for an opportune
moment to pounce
And in the valley of conflict, he sprung a rhythmic
ambush
And his bass strand was a bully that rumbled all over the
tentative lead tune
And there was a commotion and fierce rhythmic strife
And the sound of falling mountains
And the tentative tune was resilient and would not fall
And it put up a surprisingly tough fight
And it became a lone guerrilla drawing strength from
solitude ...understanding that to expect help where none
would be forthcoming was to render itself vulnerable to
tragic disappointment for, when it raised a wistful appeal
for the outside world to intervene and stop the
bully...the outside world was ruled by the bully and the
most it could do for fear of victimization was to simply
say that what was being done was wrong

And I thought of the reggae dub duets of the 80s...
Professor versus Scientist...
And I thought that we had had our own and yet not
known it
Battles of rhythm and rhyme, which had become heavy
artillery and small arms fire

And I thought that to understand *mbira*, one needs to
have grown up with the music
To have had it genetically handed over
To have had it nurtured into one's formative years
To have gone away from it in pursuit of knowledge and
another life
To have tasted the emptiness and meaninglessness of
sophistication
And then, from that projection, to be dogged by nostalgia
for things past
Nostalgia for things in the blood
To revisit the past and appreciate its values from an
elevated view
To watch the players again in memory
Watch them in their simple state... drunken from
traditional brew and happy in their own simple way

And the good music transcended my mind into memory
lane
A solitary lane one walks all alone even when in the
physical company of others
And I remembered in another time and place... a rustic
tenor that had been stalked by a rugged bass
And other sounds had whirled around those distinct two,
rising and falling with a rustic persistence
And the pattern had been a story
A plea to the spirits of the land

102

A story about trial and conviction in the village court

And a woman had danced...possessed by an ancient
spirit of the land
A time traveller from the mystic beginnings of the clan,
enjoying a moment of respite in the modern world

And in another world, so close and yet so far, she could
have turned heads
In First Street, East Gate, West Gate, Sam Levy or some
other centre of African subversion, where African people
wandered *semhuka dzakarasirirwa*,[1] possessed by the
rouged deities of Western cultures and the
meaninglessness of their so-called sophistication
And she had danced to life...whirling in a whirlpool of
African lore

And she had sung: *'Kufa kunesu machewe*
Ndakanga ndabaiwa
Kunoda vadzimu kufa kwangu'[2]

And seated, Biri naGanyira was shaking to the rhythm of
African lore
And Chief Nyandoro was being inaugurated
And armed traditional men were dancing around Tinyarei
And I was asking my grandmother *kuti*, 'Who are these
people?'
And she was saying, ''They are mediums of the heroes of
the First *Chimurenga*. No heroes of like status have
walked this land since!'

---

1. ...where black people wandered like cursed animals
2. And she had sung: *Death is with us for real/I almost got murdered*
    My death requires ancestral authority

103

The spot with rash

And when the order came, we took off and chased the
horizon right down to Wema...a disintegrating
riverfront settlement that reminded me of the Amazon
settings of the movie 'Anaconda'
Some freedom fighters were there who had left Boende
ahead of us to clear the river supply route of rebel threat

And then we took off again...this time straight for
Bokungu
And it was all swampy...Far beneath the canopy of
trees, there would be an occasional gleam of black water
that reminded us that we were not flying over dry ground

And it was treacherous terrain that bore the mark of
tragedy
The land the Belgian Leopold once called his own private
property
The land in which European champions of civilization,
Christianity, human rights, rule of law and democracy
maimed and murdered over ten million African people

And...it is said that there are places on this planet
Places that are prone to violence
Places that have seen so much death and destruction that
they are caught in a drama of death
The dead re-enacting death and destruction in the
medium of the wily living
The dead possessing the living to re-enact atrocity in a
drama that is mortally absolute

And I wondered if the Congo was one such place
A place where time was in a state of riot...
A place where progress was 'marking time' in a swirl of violence and meanness

And if this great planet were a living thing, what would the Congo be?
The spot with rash?
The spot the giant would be inclined to scratch unconsciously until he drew blood...to create a wound he would not allow to heal?
Who are those who have never had a spot of rash that felt masochistically nice to scratch?
A small wound they would not leave alone?

And, was that what the great lakes were to the planet...?
A small wound that should not be allowed to heal?
The place from which blood should be drawn to sustain the lives of Europeans in the West?
The place from which European plunderers should draw uranium with which to destroy mankind?

And, was it sheer coincidence that the uranium the plunderers used to destroy Hiroshima and Nagasaki should have been drawn from here?

And what were the implications of having such robbers walking amongst us?
Confident and without qualms?
Categorizing us into friend or foe?
Terrorists or Christians?
Legitimate or illegitimate?
All of it against a racially prejudiced datum?

And we recline in procrastination, naively imagining that
because we have not been to Pearl Harbour, so we must
be safe

But...could it be sheer coincidence that the struggle to
monopolize that by which the human race could be
exterminated...could it be sheer coincidence that such
an unholy struggle should be dramatized here...in the
cradle of human kind?

Was it sane by any standards...?
Was it human by any moral code that ownership of
resources for the manufacture of weapons of mass
destruction should even be debated...?
That it should be exclusive or even inclusive of anyone?
Or worst of all, that it should be monopolized?
Was the exclusive ownership of nuclear weapons by the
demonic raiders from the Atlantis a measure of tolerance
to those excluded from owning them?

Did populations the world over feel safe, watching
innocents being trampled to dust, sovereign governments
being deposed and puppets installed to protect minority
racist interests against majority nationalist livelihood?

Was it respect for human life?

Or was it not pre-meditated murder even before the
victim was identified?

Or were we Africans not already identified and it was
simply a matter of time before a silly excuse could be
found to demonize African self-determination as
infringing on supremacist white privilege?

Demonize African sovereignty as abusing Western white rights?

Ishango

And I stared down at the Alouette's shadow fleeting
across the equatorial jungle
And it pooled all my mind to imagine that a part of this
great jungle had witnessed the birth of writing

Ishango!

Ishango was part of this great jungle!
And it had all started here...millennia even, before the
Pharaohs and their hieroglyphics!
Seven thousand years ago, at Ishango, African people had
attempted to commit transitory orature to the
permanence of script
And the jungle down below had borne the presence of
those men who had thought big enough to want to
eternalize the record of human experience

And just what was it had been encoded in the time-
frosted notches found at Ishango?
A record of death and destruction?
A catalogue of atrocities that had started the tradition of
violence and meanness?

And I wondered what had happened to that great
civilization
Had it fleeted across African history as the Alouette's
shadow was now fleeting across the great jungle?

And I tried to divine the secrets that lay beneath the
canopy of the jungle

How many dead lay restless in these lands...stirring to the powerful sound of helicopter gunships?
How many ghosts hushed to the background sounds of this absolute theatre of war?
How many held their ethereal breath to the sporadic rattle of machinegun fire?
How many cowered from the gigantic bursts of artillery and anti-aircraft fire?

And above all, were we here as much to stop Africa bleeding as drawn by the proneness of the place to death and destruction?

Jungle drama

And through the afternoon sky, we thrust West...
Two Alouettes alone above the equatorial jungle...
A red spear thrown into the troubled great lakes by
African people of the south
A rotored spear of war... and peace too... if our punches
could tell

And I sang '*Kufa kwangu*'... my voice subdued by the
even beat of rotors
And my mind whirled into African lore
And traditional men who were the spirits of the First
Chimurenga rode the Alouette with us... their eyes fixed
north... eyes reddened *negonamombe renguva yehondo*[1]

And the beat of rotors became *mbira* sounds
And our AK47s became spears
And the two barrels of the aircraft machinegun were two
spears aimed into the enchanted jungle
And the ammunition bin was a quiver of many shining
arrows

And then we were seeing through the same eyes... feeling
and thinking with the same mind
And it was as if I had been here before... in another time
and life
And it was strange... some misted mystic working of the
mind
Was it race memory?

1.   ...Eyes reddened by wartime drug smokes

110

Had Zimbabweans come through here from the north?
And was what was happening to me now a race
recognition?
A replotting of the route of migration?

And I imagined that West of us, in Bokungu or Ikela, the
tall commando and the commando with strong hands
would be playing *Kufa kwangu* and that the helicopter
homing system would actually be homing in on the signal
of revolutionary rhythm and rhyme... the tune the
ancient ones played at the place of sorrow in the hills of
Manzou, making a last stand against white invaders

And Tinyarei sang, '*Inga zuva rabuda*[2]
Kufa kunesu machewe
Kunoda vadzimu kufa kwangu'
And a cold hand touched my neck and I turned to
look...
And it was only the intercom lead at the back of my flying
helmet

And I looked at the pilot... looking straight ahead... lost
in his own memory
And I looked at him again ... and at the booted feet on
the yaw pedals
The booted feet looked strange... almost unreal

And those feet had once been guerrilla feet, criss-crossing
Zimbabwe, fighting white colonialists and wresting the
land inch by inch from imperialist control
And now, he was doing it again... on a continental and
hi-tech scale

2. And Tinyarei sang, 'the sun has risen...

111

I wondered who he was beyond the helicopter...
Beyond the uniform and protocol of military life...
At home...
On the streets of Harare...
At the *braai* stand *kwaMereki*...[3]
In the rurals of Zimbabwe...
Or out in the farms, repossessing stolen lands from
arrogant Rhodesians

One thing I already knew...
He had been ZANLA
And I also knew that the gunner in the other aircraft had
been ZIPRA

And there were many more such men...
At Kitanda, on the eastern front, when one major frowned
at some misdemeanour during a briefing, I had
immediately recognized him as a guerrilla who had
operated in my home area. Later on, when I told him
about it, he had laughed and remarked that I must have a
very sharp memory

Now, looking at the pilot lost in memory, I wondered how
all of them must feel to know that white Rhodesians and
Western nations had supported and condoned the
Rhodesian army's partisanship to the evils of white
minority rule... I wondered how they must all feel to
know that those very same people and the invading
nations were now calling on the world to question,
condemn and punish partisanship of African armies to the
causes for which they had fought as partisan guerrilla

3. kwaMereki...(a popular drinking spot in Harare's Warren Park
    high density suburb)

112

armies... condemn African causes and yet condone their own arrogant partisanship to something disturbingly anti-black people, something that sought to relegate the black race into an economically voiceless permanent reserve labour force for white owned farms and industries...
a migrant labour force for European nations...
a menial labour force for the whole planet
A menial labour force without rights or protection

Was it fair that the world should tolerate military partisanship only when it was European armies against African people?

Should *armies of African people* that rose from voluntary guerrilla armies of *their people* that fought white armies commissioned by a supremacist white community to enforce dispossession of *African people* by white people... should those armies be demonized for supporting and enforcing repossession of stolen lands to re-empower dispossessed *Africans*?

Was it fair that the European sponsors of destabilization in Africa should be the ones to persuade African citizens to question military expenditures and ventures in reaction to such destabilization?

Was it fair that it should be European sponsors of destabilization in Africa who should clamour for sanctions against those who react to the terrorism they sponsor?

Was it fair that imperialist and capitalist Europe should ask African citizens to weigh and fear the cost of helping fellow African nations victimized by European sponsored terrorism that threatens to besiege whole regions and then ultimately recolonize the whole of Africa?

And if Zambians, Mozambicans, Ghanaians, Tanzanians,
Libyans, Cubans and the rest, had weighed and feared
the cost of sponsoring African liberation what would
have become of the yet unliberated Africa?

What would have become of Zimbabwe if Zambians and
Mozambicans had flinched from Rhodesian reprisals for
providing ZANLA and ZIPRA guerrillas with rear bases?

Was it rational even to the reasoning of imperialist
adventurers ... was it sane that Africa should just sit back
and be demonized and destabilized into a neocolonial
zombie for fear of sanctions that have always been there
in the form of sanctioned development and aid that
always came with political and economic chains?
And one wondered at the value of aid that was given
semudya ndakasungwa[4] to people with normal brains
And I wondered and wondered and wondered...
And the Alouette beat on

And, thrice we ran into rainstorms
Thrice we considered our chances
Thrice we circled warily around them...yet always back
to course and beating on
And thrice I watched the other Alouette picking pace as it
circled around a storm

And there was a predatory wariness about it...as if it
was a living beast

And I marveled, for I saw in it, a hi-tech re-enactment of
jungle drama

4.   ...aid that was given on condition of bondage...

114

And I had recognized it before, but failed to contain it in words
And it had been near a place called Katandika in Mozambique
And there had been three Alouettes
And two had pulled down to drop ammunition

And just before touch down, there had been puffs of gun smoke from the landing zones and they had flared and pulled up as vultures coming in to land on carrion would flare and pull up and away from jackals reacting to the invasion

Now I observed it again...a re-enactment of the drama of vultures, jackals and carrion
And man...
And man was the mind of the dangerous beast...
The predator killing not to devour the victim but to gain access

The concept of time

And the horizon lured us on...on an endless trail
And I wished the concept of time could be revisited and
related to activity, for, it seemed grossly unfair and
unreasonable that an hour of flying over treacherous
terrain should be equivalent in length to an hour of
commuting from Manyame Airforce Base to Highfield
township or an hour spent over a glass of beer in a bar
room
Is it fair that the hour spent in a single-engined aircraft
over equatorial swamp should be the same hour spent by
some drunken fool talking crap in a bar room?

And we thrust on...
And down below, the river Tshuapa meandered, dark and
still, like a lost entity...
Dark...serpentine...tragic, its seeming stillness belying
its speed

They said it was one of the fastest rivers on the planet

And Europeans knew about it
And they knew too about the river Congo's powerful
rush into the Atlantic
And they knew too that if a hydro-wheel were to be
deliberately entangled in the wild rush, it would be spun
to an electrical glory that could light up the African
continent to an industrial prosperity never before
witnessed on the planet
And they knew about the Congo's vast mineral reserves
and their potential to power American and European

116

nuclear and aerospace industries
And they knew about the diamonds, gold, oil and wild
game in Angola, Zimbabwe, Sierra Leone, Namibia,
Botswana, South Africa, Kenya, the DRC and the Arab
world and it irked the colonialists not used to Africans
owning anything they did not control
And it was knowledge pieced together by satellite eyes
that divined Africa's subterranean assets without Africans
knowing... and they suddenly find themselves in the
middle of civil wars sponsored to replace existing
nationalist governments not with nationalist opposition
but puppet regimes...
Puppet regimes without nationalist or liberation
orientation
Puppet individuals who would be paid to protect
European capitalist interests
Puppet regimes that would trash and erase the African
past as irrelevant to modern development

Whereas... the present is only a shadow of the past
The past inspires
The past informs
The past places the present into historical context, so that
our entry onto the scene and what we do or say is not a
magician's trick but has a bearing on what is already
there and can therefore not be viewed in isolation

The past explains violent behaviour
It explains the promiscuity of a mine town or city ghetto

The answers to who we are lie in the past and we have to
retrace our footsteps back there for orientation
It is in the past that the racial superiority and inferiority
complexes that bedevil our society today were created

and institutionalized
The imperialists who own our land and resources today
are the children of those who killed our ancestors for
them
Invaders who institutionalized the human race into
colour codes of rich and poor, angels and demons,
masters and slaves...
And it is wrong for these same people and their puppets
to be impatient with the African effort to turn the history
of our liberation into an institution to be ingrained into
the mental make-up of our children to correct the
complexes
For us to call a spade a spoon is stupid euphemism that
can only expose our children to imminent injury
Our children must know that Nehanda and her
generation unwittingly welcomed usurpers with the gift
of a black cow and they were dispossessed and slain

Our children must know that the victorious nationalists
offered the usurpers a hand of reconciliation and it was
misconstrued for weakness and nearly bitten off
Our children must know that if they do not revisit the
past they risk committing the same suicidal mistakes of
the people of old
African children must know that the bitterness, love,
hate, joy, feuds, suspicions, affluence and poverty any
people on this planet know today can be traced back into
the past...That is where curses originate and that is also
where heritage is anchored

It is in the past that one race became affluent by
dispossessing another race into destitution...not heeding
human rights to life

It is in the past that the prophet Jeremiah (31:15) heard the voice in Ramah: '...wailing and loud lamentation, Rachel weeping for her children; she refused to be consoled, because they were no more.'
And she wept in death and the God of compassion let her weep and know the healing of weeping to bereaved motherhood

It is in the past that the son of man chose the weeping place rather than succumb to the bondage of falsehood
It is in the past that the son of man rose from the dead to pursue liberation of mankind from spiritual bondage

And in the African past Nehanda chose death rather than succumb to the sacrilege of baptism by the bloodied hands of colonial priests. And she swore that her bones would rise to liberate Zimbabwe from Rhodesian evil. And in this troubled present when we stand all alone, marooned in intolerance...demonized by the dominant European world, we desperately want to believe that the God of compassion who let the spirit of Rachel, the mother of Israel weep and refuse to be consoled when her children were slain by Herod...that same God before whom we must all be equal regardless of colour...that same God of justice must have also let Nehanda's spirit weep and refuse to be consoled when her children were murdered by Rhodesians at Nyadzonia, Chimoio and Mkushi... *nekuti kuzvara kumwechete*...[1] that same God must be with us here and now in our darkest hour African children must not be misinformed that they were bought from a maternity hospital or that milk comes from a bottle

1. ...Because the pain of childbirth knows no race

The history of milk has to be traced back to the cow and the grass it feeds on and the African child's destitution must be traced back to a dispossessed ancestor and Western exploitation and indifference

African children must be informed that the corruption and destitution that bedevils Africa today are not the responsibility of the African fool alone.

They can also be traced back to European slave masters and their institutions of economic apartheid...
They can be traced back to the International Monetary Fund and the World Bank that prescribe economic remedies for African economies...calculated to derail African empowerment by punishing those who dare to challenge neocolonial dictatorship
The root of African corruption and destitution must be traced back to the architects of colonialism and apartheid who created a continent of desperate destitutes and then picked on individual destitutes and offered them a dog's place in their affluent circles in exchange for betraying the whole race
The cause of African corruption must be traced back to European and American capitalists who offer African *Neros* racist fiddles to play while Africa burns back home

African children must have the past drilled into them
They must know that the past explains and gives meaning to the present
It explains the vulnerability of African destitutes to subversion
It explains greed and selfishness
It explains the betrayal of all African revolutions into mere reform processes...all revolutionary fire corrupted

and cooled down to accommodate all the evil the people originally set out to exterminate
So that in the end, bloodied peasant revolutionaries stand back, dumbfounded, homeless, destitute and betrayed...
And they question: 'Is this what we fought for?'

The first fire

And in the distance, I saw a flicker of fire lick the jungle
from a cloud and there was smoke...
A fire in rain!

And I wondered if that was not how the first fire ever to
be lit on the planet had been made...
A design not original but incidental...
Something that must have surprised even the creator
himself

And it made me wonder how far nature goes in obeying
man-made laws of physics
Or should the question be: How accurately does man
interpret the behaviour of nature?
Are his laws just theses of convenience?
An attempt to channel or institutionalize an abstract entity
as European colonialists were attempting to
institutionalize their false sense of supremacy as human
beings and insisting on the right to determine the destiny
of African people...monitoring their constitutions, lest
they ruffle a feather and put designs to naught...or lest
they elect a wise African man in the highest office of the
land and endanger the fallacy upon which their supremacy
is founded
Is man's interpretation of nature a desperate attempt to
provisionally accommodate bits and pieces of truth until
the whole truth and nothing but the truth is found or acted
out?
An attempt to universalize occasional symmetry in a big
abstract thing...

As certain races are wont to institutionalize God...
Excluding whole races, traditions and cultures by setting
up segregatory rules for His kingdom...
Rules that make it un-Christian for African people to
notice dirt in European eyes
Rules that blow African people's reaction to dispossession
out of all proportion...turning it into biblical logs of sin
in their own eyes
Rules that create a sense of guilt in the victims, barring
them from noticing the original dispossession, which the
rules condone and diminish to trivial misdemeanors...or
specks of dust in European eyes
Rules that make it immoral and therefore unacceptable
for African people to notice and reject the injustice of
neocolonial dictatorship
Rules that are as convenient, provisional and
unattainable as the horizon is to riders of sky-horses

A destination that keeps pulling away until one abandons
the chase in death

Rear guard action

And the Alouettes beat on
Two birds of war, on the trail of a tireless horizon
Running, running and running in an hour that was as
long as an afternoon
And sometimes the horizon would hang around a column
of rain, as if for a chat, only to abandon it on our approach
And sometimes the horizon would diffuse into a shower
of rain...a smoke screen that accorded the horizon
moments of respite and time to pull dirty tricks
unobserved

And we would beat into the soft showers, visibility
reducing to zero and the horizon would not be there
And the misty rain would keep us anxious company for
moments longer than necessary...
Fighting a stubborn rearguard action for the horizon...
A celestial guerrilla terrorist, deterring our progress and
giving the horizon time to pull away

And we beat on...over uncharted territory
We beat on...westward, informed by a global
positioning system, divining directions to places lost in
the jungles of the planet

We beat on, led by the hi-tech angel of mercy clamped to
the pilot's stick and rising to the occasion inspired by a
hi-tech eye in the far sky...a satellite that scanned
heaven and earth, playing God, knowing every place
there is on the planet, giving consultation to whoever
cared to consult and leading anybody anywhere

And at last, we came to city *ya*Bokungu

And the townsfolk came to watch the landing
And the MI crews too
And the commandos who had left Boende ahead of us

And the commander, a lieutenant colonel, said, 'Had you
decided not to come?'

And the pilots said, 'No Sir. We were on our way.'

And it felt good to be together again

And we were allocated the same accommodation with the
MI crews...a war-broken house on the edge of the
jungle
And we were then taken on a tour of town

Cruel mercy

And one day a man joined us in the shade...
A fighter they said was awaiting repatriation to
Zimbabwe for habitual drunkenness

He looked sick and came drawing his stretcher bed and
weapon in the dirt

And scavengers of gossip such as are found among all
gatherings of men talked in undertones as he
approached...
And they said it never rained for the man...It always
poured

And they intimated that he had sold everything and
sneaked out of the country to the United Kingdom where
his wife was slaving and he had not been allowed to
disembark from the aircraft and his only experience of
UK had been through the misted window of the parked
aircraft through which he saw the blurred figures of self-
righteous English men and women confidently boarding
an aircraft to a Zimbabwe whose nationals a clique of
oppressors were persecuting...
Oppressors whose conscience could not be touched by
the moral awkwardness of their stance
Oppressors carrying laptops from which to demonize a
Zimbabwe they could not bear to see prosper not as their
own
Oppressors unused to African people charting their own
destiny
Oppressors illiterate to the writing on the Great Stone

Walls . . .
Notice an inexorable black consciousness flowing with the
formidable force of the Congolese river Tshuapa . . .
Notice a relentless black consciousness volcano spewing
lava of consciousness over all the dispossessed people of
the world
Notice a runaway black consciousness train running all over
colonial self-righteousness and Rhodesian arrogance

And they had come together . . . him and the oppressors
who had refused him entry into their own country
Exterminators of Irish men now indoctrinating African
people to turn the other cheek for the benefit of their
exploiters . . . so that even when denied entry into
European lands, they would gladly grant their oppressors
free entry into African lands
When demonized, they would love and pray for their
demonizers
And when dispossessed of lands and livestock, they
would give up even the freedom to chart their own
destiny
And they would want to compensate the thieves for the
recovery of stolen heritage
And even as the heads of our heroes Chingaira and
Mashayamombe lay mummified as a result of colonial
atrocities, as trophies of dispossession in the display
cabinets of museums of absolute human degradation, we
would stupidly let Cecil Rhodes and Starr Jameson, the
evil architects of our destitution rest in peace in a shrine
that is the abode of the highest spirits of the land

And the gossipers intimated that the man had returned
for duty and it was not official that he had tried to run
from the fight to repossess his own heritage

127

And disappointment had driven him to drink...wherever he found it

And now, he threw his stretcher bed and weapon on the ground
And as he fell onto the bed he said, 'I tell you *lotoko* will kill you...It is poison.'

And I looked at him and could not fathom what cruel quirk of fate drove African people to the homes of those who did not like them
What masochism attached African people to some European communities?
And those who spoke in undertones...the scavengers of gossip intimated that he had been delirious when taken in...
Delirious and talking to imaginary prostitutes at Chikwanha, in Chitungwiza, Zimbabwe.
And they had put him on a drip for three days and he was now better and probably thinking of Court Martial, loss of rank and detention in barracks plus discharge

And they said he must also be regretting everything he had pawned, including clothes he had bought for his mother and children when he missed them...
He must now be regretting having pawned them for drink

And two women came, who were selling *lotoko*
And no one would buy

And then they recognized the man on the stretcher as their good customer
And they offered him a free measure and he said, 'No ways.'

And everybody commended him for bearing the will to
fight his addiction
And they encouraged him saying, 'You should religiously
stick to your recovery plan and not give in to any
pressure...no matter how great.'

And he said, 'Never again!'
And he limped away...his denims falling
And the women went away too...disappointed

And later on we took off too...five of us...for the
Catholic mission
And, at a crossroads in the tall grass, we came upon the
man and the two women together and a half-cup of
lotoko fell from the man's hand
And he just stared at us, at a loss at what to say

And we laughed
And it was as if he was doing it for us and not for
himself
And in the distance I looked back and saw him looking
wretched, sicker and more helpless than before
And the women were no longer there

And he was standing alone...
Alone, at a crossroads that was both physical and
spiritual
Not knowing what to do
His spirit willing...but his flesh weak

And I saw in him an Africa alone, at its own crossroads
of self-determination and suicidal dependence

Should we African people be like drug addicts taking the

drug dealer's cruel mercy and living one hour at a time?
Should we have our destitution turned into a global
institution?
A United Nations Aid for Africa?
Should we have our destitution turned into a conduit of
interference, control and subversion?
A hapless victim of USAID?
Should we have our demise institutionalized into an
unjust global objective, complete with European non-
governmental organizations tasked to see things through
by prescribing retrogressive economic policies and
converting young people into puppet politicians?
All of it so that Africa remains chained to slave European
economies
Or should we pull through the darkest hour of our
history and come out reformed addicts, washed clean of
ruthless Western aid?

Did it not take Israel forty years to shake off addiction to
Egyptian slavery?
Did their dark hour not make some of them long for days
of slavery?

Was it not a dark hour and a shaking of the planet that
preceded the liberation of mankind?
And the curtain that separated the presence of God from
mankind was not pulled up but ripped apart...
And the presence of God deluged mankind, destroying
the myth that he belonged to one people

No...

The dark hour must be lived through
We cannot live thirty minutes of it and then turn back the

clock to postpone the pain into generations of our
children

No...

The savagery that has to go with liberation has to be
lived through
It is not fatherly for African men to want to commit the
future of our children into the hands of economic
oppressors
It is wrong to remain with a thorn in the foot lest its
removal cause us great pain and days of limping
It is wrong to exclusively prescribe anaesthetics to handle
the pain of a thorn in the foot

A thorn should be removed and thrown into the fire and
healing should be allowed to take its essentially unhurried
course
Anaesthetics should not be a permanent solution to pain
Anaesthetics are like European aid that creates an
imprisoning dependence

The drug addict must not accept free drugs in exchange
for abandoning rehabilitation into normal health and
normal society

Africa must reject aid that is given in exchange for
abandoning African empowerment...
Such is synonymous with voluntary imprisonment for the
sake of free food in jail

Satanic causes

And men returning from rest brought papers from home
And we devoured them for want of something to read

And there was talk in them
Talk of white European farmers calling black African
land occupiers 'invaders' and 'squatters' just as they had
called fighters for freedom and democracy 'terrorists'
And they were calling everyone to a national prayer day
for peace and order
And they were appealing to a Western international
community to intervene and install a democracy in which
a white minority would call the shots

And the naivety and self-righteousness of it all beat my
mind...
The blatant disrespect for African people and African
sovereignty
The slave-master sureness that there would be Africans
stupid enough to pray for a consolidation of their own
dispossession

But how could African people surely pray for a peace
that disadvantaged them?

How could African people join Rhodesians in prayer?
Join hands with Rhodesians who in spite of having been
forgiven for murders of African people, continued to be
boldly racist and unapologetic?
How could African people join hands with Rhodesian
barbarians who were nostalgic about days when they

could have just shot Africans with impunity?
How could African people have such short memory?

Could African people surely join hands and bow heads with oppressors who had fought tooth and nail to muzzle their voices?
Could anybody in all the world witness how many democratic elections the Rhodesians ever held in all the days of their rule?
How many national prayer days had Rhodesians and all their organizations held to appeal for divine intervention against the lawlessness and anguish of dispossession that empowered them into self-righteous acts of dispossession?
How many people did Selous Scouts kill with the blessing of an oppressor community in order to prevent true democracy?
Were any African believers in the God of Heaven...and the God of Justice stopping to think what kind of prayer that would be?
What kind of prayer could a Rhodesian community put before a God of Justice...a prayer they could not have put up when they were denying African people the right to live?

To which church would the worshippers go?
Who would lead the prayers?
What bible would be used?
Which scriptures would be quoted?
Would it be the one that says: 'Do unto others what you would have them do unto you'?

And would it not be the ultimate sacrilege for Rhodesians to use the Holy Bible and yet know that they derailed the train of democracy to institute an illegitimate Unilateral Declaration of Independence that haunted African people to death for fifteen years?

Would it not be the ultimate sacrilege to read those scriptures and yet know that they owed their affluence to the dispossession of African people?

It pooled all my imagination to think how African people could be converted enough to be part of the Rhodesian community's hypocrisy?

How could any right thinking African person be converted enough to take unholy causes to the holy Altar of God and pray that they continue to owe their livelihood to exploiters without a conscience?
How could African people feel good about committing national posterity into the hands of iniquitous aliens?

How could poor African people justify a peace that comes from acceptance of such an evil status quo?

And how would genuine worshippers justify what would happen at the close of the prayers...?
Minority white Rhodesians riding 4×4s and private aircraft to mansions on prime land
African worshippers disappearing into servants quarters or walking and commuting to locations and villages perched on broken hills in barren lands, convinced that it is better to be quiet about their poverty and landlessness in order to feed from crumbs that fall from Western corporate tables and in order to appease a European community who hold black life in such contempt that they would not send troops to stop their

kith and kin from abusing and demonizing African people

How would any genuine worshipper justify that?

The piety of men

It bothered me long after passing the paper onto others
It bothered me deep into the Congolese night...long
after everyone had gone to sleep

There was something I was failing to understand...
I was failing to understand how the African brethren's
hatred of each other could blind them to the absolute evil
of Rhodesian colonialists...blind them enough to want
to give unrepentant Selous Scouts a voice and a seat in a
government of African people against whom they had
violated all rules of combat in order to cause enough
untold pain to force them to give up resistance
And all of it because of a religious and partisan loyalty
all Rhodesians had to an apartheid system that sought to
consecrate a white-master-black-servant world order in
which Rhodesians would never die

It was unbelievable that Selous Scouts were actually
coming back...appealing to the piety and simple
reasoning of weaker men to forgive and forget the
dispossession of African people

It was unbelievable that Selous Scouts were coming
back... tasked to re-harness lost colonies and
protectorates for the economic benefit of the imperial
West

And African people were divided
And it was a case of recurrent history playing itself
out...

The betrayal of Moses by a brother Jew he was fighting
to liberate from Egyptian slavery being re-enacted in
different space and time settings
It was a case of those being liberated running to the
thrones of their apartheid masters to reverse liberation
and to consolidate their bondage
A curse of recurrent scriptures possessing liberated slaves
to stake out crucifixion crosses for their liberators

Otherwise, why were those wanting to join the prayer
initiative not questioning the moral correctness of
wanting to preserve a status quo in which Africans would
remain dispossessed and the whites unfairly empowered?
Why would they not question the selective application of
the morals of the Bible by Rhodesians who did not seem
to see the ungodliness of dispossession?

And why would the southern Rhodesian colonialist's
prayer initiative not start with remorse and confession to
crimes against humanity...
Crimes of dispossession and murder of black human beings?

Why were Rhodesians not talking about starting on a clean
slate?
And was their reluctance driven by fear of relinquishing
all the colonial loot to which they owed their affluence?

If they were truly Christian, why would they be reluctant
to relinquish everything taken by force, everything built
by forced labour and all positions and possessions
acquired not by merit but by the colour of skin?
Why were they not willing to return to Caesar what had
been taken from Caesar?

Why were they not being human enough to return the
heads of African heroes in their possession?
Heads decapitated by their ancestry purporting to
champion civilization and tolerance in Africa?

And why did the European clergy require that African
people shed their cultural heritage not into baptismal fire
but into private collections to be viewed for a price in the
natural history museums of European capitals?

Why were African people being persuaded to reject the
spirits of their liberation heroes as spirits of darkness and
yet help European people sanctify collaborating white
missionaries into saints... sanctify wolves who
blasphemed the essence of Christianity and facilitated
dispossession and murder of African people?
What kind of Christian practice beheads African fighters
against dispossession and mummifies the heads and sends
them home to be treasured as trophies of an unjust war?
They did that to Chingaira
They did that to Mashayamombe
They are holding onto those heads to this day
Enjoying and treasuring and preserving African people's
pain and bereavement...
Sanctioning its expenditure for special occasions of
absolute sadism when they sit alone in the capitals of
Europe, discussing Africa in the absence of Africans,
plotting her destitution... wary for any signs of
awakening...
Was it a stubborn reluctance to let go of the slave... even
in death?

But, would the God of Justice who blessed the champions
of Jewish liberation from Egyptian slavery deal differently

with the champions of African liberation from British
barbarism?
Would He reject the moral righteousness of African
heroes' fury at dispossession and commit them to penance
for rejecting the sacrilege of baptism by wolves in sheep's
clothing?

No...

Black people must refuse to look at religion the way
Bible-toting Western imperial agents would want us to
look at it...
It would only cloud our reasoning around sin and eternal
penance

Why for instance should the idea of hell not be as fearful
to Rhodesians as they have made it feel to African
people... especially after all the evil they have
perpetrated on Africa?
Why should the idea of hell make any sense at all when
the preachers of that gospel are not afraid of divine wrath
for murdering African people?
Is the idea not a gross violation of divine poetic justice
that must be the essence for God to forgive an oppressor
for the evils that have given us destitution and conversely
given him affluence?

How could we surely be poor and landless and yet know
that our fathers owned rich and fertile lands that are still
there and yet still occupied by the people who enslaved
and killed them in order to build their affluence on
African sweat and blood?
We sit back and watch them pass our rich heritage from
one generation of self-righteous usurpers to the next

while we pass legacies of poverty from one African
generation to the next!
African people must never look at religion the way
Europeans want them to look at it
African people could forgive but never ever forget the
cause of their destitution before correcting it

The God of heaven and earth...
The God of justice cannot demonize fighters for
liberation from apartheid
It is not true
There is no moral righteousness in compensating the
robber children of Satan
There is no godliness in legitimizing and sanctifying
ownership of a stolen heritage

African people must know that it is not fair for them to
go to church to help spiritualize their destitution into a
divine cross to be borne without complaining
African people should refuse to watch their grim life
being spiritualized into a Dolorrossa[1] to the place of the
skull...
Watch the path of their lives being narrowed to the
weeping place

Why must we forget that we are destitute because British
and American champions of democracy and rule of law
watched with indifference while African people were
being brutally dispossessed and denied democracy by
their satanic kith and kin?

---

1. Dolorrossa was the road to Calvary where Jesus was crucified.
   Calvary was also called *the Weeping Place* or *Place of the Skull*

We should not advocate for an impoverished peace and silence inspired by a religious humility custom-made for us alone

As the guerrilla leader said in 79, African people must not want peace at all cost

Africa must go only for an honourable peace
A Landed peace!

I thought that if Africa has to turn to religion, then let it be to uphold the old Law of Moses

Let Africa disgorge the eyes of those who disgorged African eyes

The curse of the freed slave

And the next day I awoke at dawn
Awoke to bitter introspection
A brutal self-analysis that ruthlessly questioned values I
had never questioned before

I looked into the tragic irony of destiny and for the first
time felt the curse of observation which The Preacher
must have felt as he meditated on the sad business that
God gave the sons of man to be busy with

I wondered if it was the curse of nature that the freed
slave should not know what to do with freedom

Was it the curse of nature that after a fight to death for
freedom, a victorious slave must go back to the
vanquished slave-master for instructions on how to carry
on?

Was it the satirical irony of nature that made a victorious
slave beg for reconciliation with the vanquished slave
master?
Was it paranoia at being left alone without anyone to
look up to . . . ?
Someone to give them the day's programme?

Was it characteristic of freed slaves to fear the
responsibility of having to make their own decisions?
Were the murmurings against Moses on the road from
Egypt through the desert a condition of all enslaved people
of the world that made slavery viewed in retrospect seem

better than the desert walk to freedom?

When I went to pee on the grass, I looked into the meshed
jungle and wondered what unfortunate condition of
destiny attached liberated men to former tormentors as
dogs attached themselves to cruel masters

What made weak men seek the cruel friendship of their
oppressors?
What made African people seek the approval of
Rhodesian imperialists?
What made African people put their trust in Selous
Scouts who never forgave them for establishing African
rule in less time than Ian Smith's projected thousand
years?

What made African people trust or even talk to Selous
Scouts who impersonated freedom fighters in order to
commit gruesome atrocities which when blamed on
freedom fighters would trash the people's revolution into
a directionless bloodbath?
What made Zimbabweans let Cecil Rhodes and Jameson,
the racist architects of our destitution rest in peace in our
land whilst in Britain the heads of Mashayamombe and
Chingaira lay mummified in displays of racial hate as
human trophies of a mutilation of human civilization
A mutilation of the right to a decent death and burial
A mutilation of international justice, democracy, rule of
law and human dignity, which a whole biased Western
world was refusing to see

I awoke to questions and questions and questions...

About trees and men

And it bothered me even when it became Sunday...the
day they called the Lord's Day
And I was wondering that if the God of Heaven existed, as
we believed he did, why would he not rent the global
racial curtain that separated African people from the
riches of the planet...even in their own lands...?
Why would he not rent it to bless African people with the
blessing of economic empowerment?
Why would he not let the consciousness of African
empowerment rage across the planet to all the
dispossessed and dislocated people of the world...to
South Africans, Namibians, Kenyans, Asians, Arabs,
South Americans and to the bottom of the world where
British convicts were holding Aborigines hostage below
the celestial ship's deck?

And we went to church...
A conglomeration of buildings that stood incongruously
intact amidst ruins of war and lawlessness
And I observed that the Congolese had their own style of
Christianity...
A Catholicized or Westernized tradition...

And then it was not exactly like that either
There was something in the way they practised
religion...
Something one felt rather than reasoned...
Something one could not put a finger on
Something that refused to be completely enveloped or taken
over

144

Something that demanded to be Congolese...

The Madonna on the walls of the church was a tall
Congolese woman wrapped in *liputa*...
And the Romans too
And the people who condemned a black Jesus

And the songs and drums were Catholic and yet also *rumba*
And the dance was Catholic and yet also the *kwasa-
kwasa* dance

And I had observed an intangible something in the way
the women danced at Boende and it was here too
And it was beautiful
And there was a woman...
A woman who read the scriptures
A woman so strangely beautiful she looked divine

And at that moment, in the presence of God or so I
believed, I saw that, black, which some fools regarded
with negation had a beauty all its own...
A beauty so extraordinarily the real thing it was a
tangible statement of the divine abstraction of God

I saw that black had power and presence and glory
whose recognition did not need the endorsement of
another race on the planet

And it felt strangely nice, listening to the readings yet not
understanding a thing

And it was a wonder how sometimes when learning a
new language, one understood only those speeches
directly addressed to one

And when church service was over, I stood outside
church...I stood by a man-made mount with a cavern in
which stood the figure of a white Madonna

And I was attracted to it by a big *mutsamvi* tree on the
mount
And it was a big tree with massive roots that reached
over the boulders of the mount to burrow into the earth
beyond
And it appeared like a conscious effort telling the story of
the struggle of trees...
A struggle being re-enacted by African people fighting to
find anchor in the land on the premise that it is
ownership and therefore anchor in land that stabilizes
and gives substance to a people's sovereignty
Because sovereignty that is devoid of land ownership is
superficial and liable to dislocation because it is
unanchored by the life-giving earth on which people
build homes and live and draw means of livelihood
Because life-sustaining resources are found in the land
and whoever owns the land controls life and is
empowered by such ownership to exploit the resources
for development
Because native ownership of the land empowers natives,
anchors as well as gives substance to any development,
while on the other hand, ownership of land by an alien
capitalist minority is a recipe for neocolonial dictatorship
It makes all development provisional and subject to the
whims of materialists insensitive to the real needs of
natives
Because European owners of African land will not grow
African staple foods if it becomes more profitable or
politically expedient not to do so

Because European commercial farmers of African land
will not grow maize if it nurtures their egos to see
African people starve and blame landless African
governments for famine

I read the story of the trees like print
I saw that in the beginning trees must have had roots as
their only defence
They must have, like man, recognized the importance of
the land to their livelihood
And they had burrowed into the earth in search of
nourishment and they had clutched at particles of earth
and rock in anchor against dislocation
But human and animal predators had come and
consumed the trees to sustain their own lives
And after that first defeat, the next generation of trees had
come camouflaged and armed with thorns to reclaim lost
territory
And some, like cacti carried their own water in order to
survive the most hostile of conditions in the Great War
And in like fashion African liberation guerrilla armies
had carried light weaponry that created liberated zones
inaccessible for exploitation by the enemy

And they were still reclaiming lost territories...
And in Great Zimbabwe, the fight was to the death
And colonial predators were panicking and enlisting all
nations of the world to combine their foul breath in order
to blow out the powerful light of justice

Unempowered choice
is not freedom

And even when it was night again, I kept thinking about
the story of trees and African people and African
politicking distorted by foreign languages

I thought about land and how it anchors people and
development

And I thought about the confusion back home...
The confusion about democracy, good governance and
land

And I thought about partisan guerrilla armies coming
home with political independence and everybody taking
the benefits without questioning the partisanship of those
heroes

And I thought about democracy and how it cannot exist
beyond the electoral process unless it is based on
empowerment of people to give them a real economic
voice and not just the electoral right to choose who
among the elite, the most aggressive or the foreign-
sponsored has to dictate to them

That night at Bokungu, I saw that it is not democracy to
simply have peace and freedom of speech, movement and
association... and to be employed by white people
I saw that it is not democracy to have the right to life and
shelter and education and health when people do not

have land on which to move and associate freely...
Land on which to build homes...
Homes from which to build healthy, meaningful and
confident lives

I saw that it is not democracy to have the right to life and
yet not have land from which to draw the livelihood

I saw that it is not democracy to have choice and yet not
be empowered to pursue the choices

I thought that democracy must go beyond choice of
government

Democracy must be founded on economic empowerment
of the majority

Choice alone without empowerment undermines the
decisions of a destitute majority and in postcolonial
Africa, it compromises and subjects African people to the
whims of an affluent white minority that has no loyalty
to African causes

African people should be empowered to pursue and
realize the ideals of the democracy for which they vote

What surely is the good of having the right and freedom
to eat anything one wants to eat and yet not have the
food or the land on which to grow it?

Do those who fancy themselves champions of democracy
really believe in all earnest that African people should
really buy their idea of an African democracy in which
destitute African people have the right to choose while

rich capitalists and imperialists hold the key to the
realization of those choices?

African power should not come in quarters
African power should not be shared with aliens who have
foreign loyalties because that would be synonymous with
the Babylonian giant Nebuchadnezzar standing on feet of
clay and iron[1]
A giant that cannot stand the test of time

The surrogate giant with feet of clay must be bludgeoned
to dust and real life fleshed and breathed into the bones
of African liberation heroes so that a new power is
created that is not split between racial, economic and
political lines

And then all power should be one
And it should be African power unadulterated by
Western interference
And it should never die

---

1. An allusion to Nebuchadnezzar's dream in the Old Testament,
    Daniel 2 Vs 31–45.

The beauty of imperfection

And at Ndjili International Airport, Kinshasa, I stood
alone in a crowd of armed men awaiting the flight back
home

And I desperately missed Tinyarei, wanting to hold her as
only a man can hold a woman
I desired to look at her across a crowded waiting room
and to enjoy the romance of recognition and the urgency
of desire thereafter

And we waited to go home
And we waited many days

And on another day...a rainy dawn unlike any other
Congolese dawn I had ever known, I washed my face from
the mainplane run-off of a parked Ilyushin thinking
nothing

And then after a long, long time, looking at the frosted
lights of Kinshasa, across the dip where the first fight
took place and the forces of neocolonial retrogression
were pushed back, I desired to have Tinyarei and
thought that one day I must ask her how it feels to a
woman, to know that she is desired
Today, I really think it is crucial that black men must
know what pleases black women, just as it is critical
today that that certain white people must be taught that
black people are real human beings...real flesh and
blood
Just as it is critical today that huge sections of the

152

American and European white community must know
how it feels like to be a black man, being short-changed
every time... a black person whose self esteem has to be
dragged and soiled in racist murk and the shame and
woes of intolerant patronization

And on another day, I had a strangely curious feeling...
A romantic stubbornness that desperately missed and
desired human contact...
A faceless black female human being
Not the spotless Western plastic model with false teeth,
false lashes, false nails, false hair, false complexion and a
false voice but a genuine feminine person with human
faults... natural and unschooled in superficial social
etiquette
Not a masculine feminist who ends up being neither man
nor woman

I wanted to touch and to hold and to shake a work
hardened hand and not the cosmetic-softened hand of the
superficial class
I wanted to feel a suckled breast and to kiss a milk-
seasoned nipple to life
I wanted to caress a cellulite-rippled bottom and to enjoy
the absolute beauty of imperfection
I wanted not the business brusqueness and practiced
throw of the prostitute but the genuine movements of
natural congress...
A stiffening of toes in erotic mindlessness
A shuddering in multiple orgasm
A mutual understanding to fulfill human need as only a
man and a woman can...
A man and a woman genuinely needing each other
outside the courts of law... uninfluenced by third parties

and free from a world that has institutionalized and put
guidelines to loving

I did not want to read notes on how to achieve sexual
fulfillment lest I reduce natural intercourse to an academic
course
No...
Not if I could tap from nature and instinct

And on another day, I got drunk...
And I started thinking that I was Africa
And that I was all the black people in the whole world
And that I was sick...
And that all the so-called right-thinking doctors in all the
world wished me dead
And I was believing that it was wrong as some people
insisted...it was naïve to expect to be nursed back to
health by those who wished me dead
And I was remembering that my mother had warned me
not to be polite enough to accept a poisonous gift
And I was also thinking that if all the right-thinking
doctors in all the world wished me dead, then I should
not go to them
I should go to the unorthodox healer and be made well
again just like an Africa haunted to destitution by
orthodox European designed economic recovery
programmes must go it alone...An Africa that must do
something unorthodox to be well again

I was thinking that there must surely be a time when all
popular medicine was unorthodox...
And all normal people went to the rootsman who
believed that the best medicines were prescribed by
nature...

And the rootsman was the orthodox practitioner

And the unorthodox had demonized the rootsman and
popularized their own methods...
And the unorthodox had become the orthodox
practitioners

And the rootsman who had sustained human health from
creation to the time of popular medicine by prescribing
from nature was frowned upon into anonymity, to
practice behind the scenes, handling the difficult cases of
madness, which popular medicine in all its sophistication
could not handle
And those who were healed were summoned by the high
priests of exploitation and threatened not to reveal by
whose hand they had been healed
And I thought that I should rip the curtain that hid the
powerful rootsman and his homegrown solutions in order
to fill African people with a healing consciousness
I thought that for a long, long time and I must have
dozed because I came to with a start and I was thinking
that Africa must do something unorthodox

I was thinking that Africa must pluck out the false heart
that was planted in her bosom by those who facilitated
the dispossession of her children
She must reject the fake transplant and taste the real
unorthodox beauty of life without a fake heart

And great Zimbabwe too, for 'Thou art not least' among
the nations of this planet
Zimbabwe must do something unorthodox
Zimbabwe must disinter the devil's grave that defiles the
highest shrine of the land

African people must disinter the racist grave and turn the
racist contents over to gluttonous hyenas of the wild
Gluttonous hyenas that are cursed with both organs
Gluttonous hyenas that haunt the African night, ridden
by African witches
Gluttonous hyenas whose laughter derides the moon
The moon that circles warily around the planet making a
tidal effort to rob the planet's oceans dry, in order to
drench its own arid surface
The moon that haunts the planet's canine life
I thought all that and it was madness
And I had never known that madness could feel so
strangely beautiful
So astonishingly the perfect thing
So superlatively divine

A viral memory

And, very often, I missed Mami...
Interchangeably with Tinya
On the stretcher bed
Marooned in memory
Unconsciously caressing the cold steel of my weapon
I missed Mami with religious wretchedness
Wanting her by my side
Wanting to feel the rustle of her breath against my cheek

On her Congolese cane bed, when I had turned so she lay on
top of me, she had chuckled...a discordant Congolese
laughter...
I missed the sound...wondering how long I would be
able to retain it recognizable in the vaults of my
memory...
Accessing it secretly...
Treacherously replaying it again and again against every
possible background...
An orgasmic catalyst treacherously catalyzing climax with
another woman
A viral memory, severely crippling future relationships by
comparison

How often would I miss her...?
Alone, on a bar room stool, sipping a beer?
How often...?
Above the equatorial jungle, lulled by the even beat of
rotors?
At home, in the crew room, spicing the escapade into an
epic romance?

Her hips had looked and felt firm and very real against mine ...a carving of flesh and blood...unbelievably available

I missed that too...
And the smell of woman about her...
Innate...
Unperfumed

I had learnt to smell and appreciate feminine scent when I was a child...
An older cousin used to cuddle me and it had felt so nice to snuggle into her and be tickled into pleasant laughter...enjoying the cologne God had intimated into womanhood to charm men into conjugal union

And then it had bound me to Tinyarei
And at Bokungu I had smelt it in the woman who had done the readings in church
She had said *'Mbote'* as she passed by my side and a pleasant confusion had seized me...A scented confusion...

And later on when I was reviewing it in bed, I had told myself, 'No chance...the competition is too stiff.'

And I had remembered the rough crew room talk at home when someone had said, 'A woman with good assets is disadvantaged in wartime. She is conspicuous and vulnerable to lechery and abuse. Those she will not accept under normal circumstances will have her by duress of arms. Any armed rogue can have her.'

I had remembered

And I had winced
And I had turned
And for the first time I had seen where a cluster of six
bullets had entered the broken house through a door
panel

And I had read the story...
A non-verbal cryptic script...
Three of the bullets had cratered the opposite wall and
two had left through a window pane...too fast to take it
apart

Had the sixth bullet found its target...slamming him
against the wall and spattering it with his warm blood
where the wall appeared scrubbed around another crater?

A commando warrant officer had spoken of scrubbing
blood from the broken house and I had felt invisible eyes
on me
And I had wondered if the war-dead ever really left the
theatre of war
Did they not hang around in a spiritual existence
concurrent with ours...?
Living with us in broken houses...
Walking and flying with us...
No longer bitter enemies but paranormal audience
amused by sterling effort to get and preserve things that
could not be spirited with us into eternity to be ours
forever and ever

And then I always wondered if I would ever see Mami
again...?
A surprise meeting out of the blue...
On some strange street in a strange town...

Kana pachibhorani kwaMuda...A memento gleaned out
of war rubble by a lovelorn rustic war veteran

Or, would I one day turn on a bar room stool and find
her to be the woman sitting next to me...?
Powdered...
A Congolese sex worker
Her femininity irretrievably compromised, corrupted and
commercialized by war...
No longer lovable
No longer companionable beyond sexual commerce

Or, would it be in another time and life...?
As time travellers incarnated into another struggle...
Dying and being reborn
Dying and being reborn
Dying and being reborn
Trapped in the atrocious destiny of the Great Lakes
Caught in an eternal drama of death and destruction

Mukombe weropa

(Cup of blood)

And behold, Ndjili became Manzou

And men congregated in war council
Traditional men and sons of the soil, armed with
assegais, knobkerries, battle axes, bows and arrows and
an old hunter's rifle

And there were others, but not totally strange men
Men from across the oceans...
Bloodied men, dragging broken chains but still manacled
And they wanted a voice in council
And all were African men
And I said to my grandmother 'Are these people living?'
And she said, 'They are the heroes of old... coming back
to be killed again... to be betrayed by your treacherous
generation... *Makonyora!*'[1]

And there was a light drizzle
And the drizzle became *mbira* sounds
And throughout the night, the sounds drizzled and
drizzled and drizzled

A continuous filter of rhythm from the mists of African
antiquity
And there was a fire

1.   Traitors!

162

And around the fire, traditional men played the music,
drunken from traditional brew

And the spirits of the First *Chimurenga* danced
And Tinyarei sang: *Kufa kunesu machewe*
                   Tarisai ndaitwa mukomberanwa garira
                   noko

And a cup was being passed around
And an old man in folded trousers and toting an old
hunter's rifle touched it and cried: '*Hai! Yowe-e maiwe-
e!*'[2]
And he turned on his heel
And Tinyarei wept...
A mournful sound that haunted the night
And Biri naGanyira said, 'Do not do that...what is this
now? Any problem can be talked over!'

And I touched the cup

And it was the truth
And it was terribly beautiful...
And it bore the magical beauty of historical hamartia
And my grandmother cried, 'Throw it away!'

And the *mbira* sounds became the thudding of guns
And the smoke of fire was the smoke of gunpowder
And the tendrils were the spirits of war

And then I saw a village *ku*Dande...
Men filtering in from the war...

2. A distress call for mother.

Beaten men...

And my grandfather was not among them
Some men had seen him fall...dusted by an enemy's
bullet

And in Mbembesi, 'carrion men lay groaning for burial.
And the foul deed smelt above the earth.'[3]

*Ku*Mhondoro, Mashayamombe was dead and his head
taken

*Ku*Harare, Nehanda was adjourning the struggle in
martyrdom

*Ku*Manzou men were playing *Kufa kwangu*
And the message was: 'Do or die'

And the mournful sound came again
And it was Tinyarei weeping
And she was refusing to be consoled for her children
were going to be duped and slain again

And the sound was a siren that lured fallen heroes to war
council in a game of resurrection, possession and
reorganization
And they were resurrecting...the men of old
Some coming from the south with short stabbing spears
Some coming from the north, riding camels
Some coming from the northeast...tall men striding
across the African savanna

3. Allusion to Mark Anthony's lamentation after the murder
of Julius Caesar

And the men played on
And the tune was a story
And the story was about land and about life
And the story was about tolerance and racist predation
Violent racist guests dispossessing and murdering tolerant
African hosts
Racists demonizing repossession of stolen heritage
And I stood entranced by the tragic beauty of historical
hamartia
And a gun trailed me
A cocked weapon and a trigger finger taking up the slack
And the cup was being passed around
And my grandmother cried: 'Toss it to the ground!'

And the regal old man in folded trousers looked at the
cup and cried: '*Hai! Hai! Yowe-e amaiwe-e!*'
And Tinyarei wept
And Biri naGanyira was shaking to the rhythm of African
lore
And consultation was in session
And she was saying, 'If you let the spirit of war get
amongst you, you will only have yourselves to blame...
Do not drink from their cup
It is a cup of blood
And it will not get you far'

And men and women of old whispered into her ear
And they were the founders of Great Zimbabwe

And she said, 'When African people are one, all war will
be civil war
So, do not let the spirit of war get amongst you because if
you do, you will only have yourselves to blame.'
And she became foul mouthed at the new generation

165

And *mbira* sounds rose and drowned her voice
And she raised her voice above the music and cried,
'*Vana venyoka!*'[4]
And her eyes were fixed beyond the gathering

And behold, African funeral men wrestled the cup from
our hands and drank
And it was a cup of blood
And the night was 'Aho-o-o-o!' with hyena laughter
An invasion of predatory canine chaos
A snapping of canine treachery and conspiracy

And I came to...
And it had been so terrifyingly real!

And it was afternoon
And an Ilyushin came to take us home
A massive craft riding infinitely less dense medium

4. 'Serpent children!'

A matter of technique

And from the Ilyushin, going back to Tinyarei, I watched
a hazy Africa down below

And I started thinking about the Ilyushin and all it had
done for us and I was awed
And I thought that the builder of the Ilyushin must be a
big man
A big man who thought big
A big man who thought whatever he wanted to think
A big man who never sought the opinion or approval of
those who wished him ill
A big man with big intentions
A big man with the good nature of ten good-natured men
A good natured man who must have smiled at the wind
and convinced it that the effort required to bear a load
was relative to technique and with the right approach
even the heaviest of loads could be kid stuff
And the wind had agreed and borne the massive Ilyushin
on delicate hands

And all the sceptics of the world ... all the sceptics and ill-
wishers who had formed theories of failure and waited to
see the massive aircraft crash to the ground were put to
shame

And I was awed
And I thought that as it was with wasps and caterpillars
bigger than their size
So it should also be with aircraft and wind and men and
nations and the universe ...

So it should also be with Zimbabwe
And with Africa

African people must know that it must be a matter of
technique to carry a demonized Zimbabwe and a
beleaguered Africa to independent prosperity

African people must know that sometimes it is fine to be
mad

African people must know that a madness they believe in
must be a fine madness

A VERY FINE MADNESS

Glossary

Braai: a Southern African term for barbequed meat

Changamire: title of traditional ruler. Also a term of reverence

Chimurenga: a national struggle. Chimurenga is derived from Murenga, the spiritual godfather of the nation of Zimbabwe. The First Chimurenga against colonial occupation was in 1896

Fra: local shortened name for Congolese Francs

Hai! Yowe-e maiwe-e: a distress call for mother

hapana akambotaura kuti yaive nhumbu yemabhinya: nobody ever mentioned that it was a terrorist-rape pregnancy

Inga zuva rabuda / **Kufa kunesu machewe** /
Kunoda vadzimu kufa kwangu:
Look, the sun has risen / And death is still with us for real / My death requires ancestral authority

Kana pachibhorani kwaMuda: or even by the borehole at Muda

*ku*Dande: in Dande

Kufa kwangu: my death

Kufa kunesu machewe / **Ndakanga ndabaiwa** /
Kunoda vadzimu kufa kwangu:
*Death is with us for real / I almost got murdered /
My death requires ancestral authority*

Kufa kunesu machewe / Tarisai ndaitwa mukomberanwa garira noko: Death is with us for real / Look I am besieged

kuti chii chainge chapinda muvana vaMhofu: what had gotten into African children

kuti kana ini ndava kukurira ndinobatwa, asi kana ndichirohwa hapana anobata?: that I should be held back when I am winning whereas when I am losing nobody holds the enemy back?

kuti kusina amai hakuendwi: the place without maternal protection should be avoided

kuti: 'Unomupei...?': 'What can you offer her...?

kuti vatore mapfumo nenduni kubva muchengo chemba: to take assegais and knobkerries from their huts

kwaChiweshe: in Chiweshe

kwaMereki: at Mereki ...(a popular drinking spot in Harare's Warren Park high density suburb)

kwasa-kwasa: Congolese dance to Ndombolo music

'Leki nangai ... kombo naye Mami.': 'My young sister ... her name is Mami.'

Liputa: wrapper

Lotoko: an illicit highly alcoholic home brew

Makonyora: traitors

Mambaras: crooked people

maoko (maboko): hands

masangambila wine: palm wine

mbira: An ancient traditional musical instrument, the music from the instrument is also called *'mbira.'*

Mbote?: How are you?

Meso (*miso*): eyes

Mukombe weropa: cup of blood

Mwindi waNzambe: 'Light of God'

Ndombolo: Congolese rhumba music

negonamombe renguva yehondo: from wartime drug smokes

nekuti kuzvara kumwechete: because the pain of childbirth knows no race

Neros: derogatory term for corrupt leaders, alludes to Nero the eccentric and sadistic first century Roman Emperor

nyama: meat

Nyika ino ndeyeropa muzukuru: Precious blood was shed for this land

Pachibhorani kwaMuda / Kubanya kwaNyandoro: At the borehole at Muda / At the rain shrine at Nyandoro

pasina aidzora mumwe: with no one calling for reason

Peelot: *Congolese* colloquial corruption for 'pilot'

Povo: Portuguese term for the general masses popularized by the Zimbabwean Freedom fighters in Mozambique.

rurimi (*lolemu*): tongue

semhuka dzakarasirirwa: like cursed animals

semudya ndakasungwa: aid that is given on condition of bondage...

Takawira Muchineripi: The name is an allegory. Takawira defines colonial bondage. Muchineripi is a verbal challenge to a beaten enemy if he still has anything else to say.

Tinyarei: The name is also allegorical. It means: Give us a break.

tsapata (tsapato): feet

Vamwe vachiri kufamba pamusoro penyika ino / Nevamwe vane tsoka dzakadzima: Some still walking the land / And others who have passed on

Vana venyoka: serpent children

ZANLA, ZIPRA, ZNA: The armed liberation struggle for Zimbabwe was waged by two main political parties that constituted a Patriotic Front. They were ZANU (Zimbabwe African National Union) and ZAPU (Zimbabwe African People's Union)

ZANU was led by the current president of the Republic of Zimbabwe, Robert Gabriel Mugabe. Its armed wing was ZANLA (Zimbabwe African National Liberation Army)

ZAPU was led by the late vice president of the republic, Dr Joshua Nkomo. Its armed wing was ZIPRA (Zimbabwe People's Revolutionary Army)

After the war, ZANLA, ZIPRA and the Rhodesian army formed the Zimbabwe National Army (ZNA) and Airforce of Zimbabwe (AFZ) jointly known as the Zimbabwe Defence Forces (ZDF)

'Zvemweya yerima ndizvo zvatisiri kuda kumbonzwa': 'We do not want to hear anything about the spirits of darkness'